## MARRIED BUT AVAILABLE

Abhijit Bhaduri (http://abhijitbhaduri.com) has led HR (Human Resources) teams in several organizations including Microsoft, PepsiCo, Colgate and Tata Steel. He worked in South Asia and in the US for many years before returning in 2005 to work again in India. He has been a radio jockey and hosted shows in India and the US and has also dabbled in amateur theatre. He can be reached at abhijitbhaduri@live.com

# MARRIED BUT AVAILABLE

## ABHIJIT BHADURI

HarperCollins *Publishers* India
*a joint venture with*

New Delhi

First published in India in 2008 by
HarperCollins *Publishers* India
*a joint venture with*
The India Today Group
Text and illustrations on p. 43, 50 © Abhijit Bhaduri
Illustrations on p. 123, 141 © Uma Gautam

ISBN: 978-81-7223-766-0

2 4 6 8 10 9 7 5 3

**HarperCollins *Publishers***
A-53, Sector 57, NOIDA, Uttar Pradesh – 201301, India
77-85 Fulham Palace Road, London W6 8JB, United Kingdom
Hazelton Lanes, 55 Avenue Road, Suite 2900, Toronto, Ontario M5R 3L2
*and* 1995 Markham Road, Scarborough, Ontario M1B 5M8, Canada
25 Ryde Road, Pymble, Sydney, NSW 2073, Australia
31 View Road, Glenfield, Auckland 10, New Zealand
10 East 53rd Street, New York NY 10022, USA

Typeset in 10/13 Euclid
Jojy Philip New Delhi - 15

Printed and bound at
Thomson Press India Ltd.

*To Baba Ma*

# Acknowledgments

I want to use this space to vent about the plight of writers of sequels. Damned if you do and damned if you don't. Here is the problem. If the sequel turns out to be just like the first one, then there is a bunch of cribbers who will say, 'You are a one-trick pony. Why could you not write in a style that is different from the first? A sequel gives you a chance to break the mould. You have not done that. You have stuck to a formula that has worked and you are not taking risks.'

If you try to be innovative and write a sequel that is … well… different, then the same set of cribbers will find something else to be unhappy about. This time they will say, 'You disappoint me. You know this is a sequel. It is supposed to read like the first book. Why could you not make this look and feel like *Mediocre But Arrogant*?'

I asked Rascal Rusty what I should do. Rusty chewed on his unlit cigar, scratched his beard and stared into space. After a while he broke his silence.

'You should de-sequelize this book. Just tell people it is not a sequel - it is the second book in the series. This can be the M-B-A series. After *Mediocre But Arrogant*, you should call this one *Married But Available*.'

'What if I write yet another novel?'

'Then you should call it *Middle-aged But Active*.'

'What if I wanted to take risks and be innovative and break the mould?'

'Then call it *Mould Broken Again*. Stick to the M-B-A framework.'

I have taken Rusty's advice. So I am careful not to call this a sequel. It is the second book in the series. The title remains what Rusty suggested.

To my wife Nandini, and our children Eshna and Abhishek, I want to say thank you for giving me the time and space to chase every dream.

The readers of *Mediocre But Arrogant* formed a community on Orkut and invited me to join them. I thought I should leverage collective wisdom to figure out where the story should take Abbey. What happens to him in the corporate world? What would his first decade in corporate India be like? I want to say thank you to all my readers for sharing with me stories from their personal and professional lives, complete with their hopes and dilemmas. Thank you for giving me that privilege.

I want to acknowledge the ideas and suggestions of my friends and colleagues who shared their insights with me. They helped enrich my story. In particular, I wish to thank Anand Naik (ITC), Navnit Singh (Heidrick & Struggles), Madhukar Sharma (Ecoventures), Pavan Bhatia, Sucheta Govil and Kimsuka Narsimhan (PepsiCo) and Venkat Shankar (iLabs) for their suggestions. A big thank you to my multifaceted artist and poet friend Uma Gautam for bringing to life Keya's sketches. And to Rajesh R. (my ex-colleague from PepsiCo) for the photos I have used on my website banner and in this book.

Thanks, too, to Shuka Jain for the cover design and to my editor V.K. Karthika, who worked with her team at HarperCollins to bring this book to you.

# ONE

Some things have changed. Some things never will – not in this lifetime. I look at my face in the mirror of the guesthouse of my alma mater and try to discover the changes. I've just stepped out of the shower and am buttoning the black Polo shirt that has always been my favourite. The faded pair of Levis and black blazer complete the look. I shave and dab on some cologne. Like the scouts will tell you, 'Be prepared'. Then I comb my hair and, looking at the strands of silver that have appeared of late around my sideburns, wonder idly if any girl would still find me attractive. After all, at age thirty-five the girls on the MIJ campus will probably find me too old, unless I meet one of those who find older men sexy because they have grey sideburns.

The guesthouse is part of the new Executive Development Centre that the Management Institute of Jamshedpur is known for. It's built like a five-star hotel, complete with a beautiful swimming pool and a poolside bar which has been featured in several issues of the *Business Magnate*.

As I bend down to tie my shoelaces, I try and think of one good reason why Father Hathaway allowed it to be built at all, but I can't think of any.

There is one thing I do know: I hate these alumni meetings.

'You look just the same.'

'I'd never have recognized you. You've gone totally bald.'

'I've put on so much weight. The travel and eating out is killing me. So who did you marry?'

Ten years ago when I left the Management Institute of Jamshedpur as a freshly minted MBA, I never imagined that I would come back under these circumstances. I prayed during the train journey to Jamshedpur that I would not bump into a known face. God was kind. The AC chair car of Ispat Express was clearly not a popular choice with the alumni.

The knock on the door is discreet. I open the door and find a young lady smiling at me. She is wearing a formal skirt and jacket. Her shoulder-length hair has been shampooed and brushed till every strand is neatly in place.

'Hi, I am Cauvita.' She offers me a business card.

'Hi. I'm Abbey.' I look at the card. 'President of the Students' Association? Cool.'

'That's me. And here's your welcome gift.'

I open the gift-wrapped photo frame and look at the collage of familiar faces. It brings back memories that had begun to fade.

'That's Rusty. I hope he manages to come from Dubai.

That's Gur standing next to Neetika. They are married. Gur is bursting at the seams now. You wouldn't recognize him. That's Pappu… my roommate in the first year. We were in Room 208, which overlooks Daadu's Dhaba. Pappu is the craziest roomie anybody could have. He sleeps more than any other human being on the planet. Still does.'

'There were eight girls in your batch. How many of them got married to their batchmates?'

I sidestep the question and say, 'Can we go and sit on the steps of the auditorium?'

'Sure,' she says. 'I don't mind.'

I lock the door behind me and we set off.

'Is it still considered cool, going for a walk to the banks of the Subarnarekha?'

'Oh, I love watching the sunset from there. And look, it's a full moon night.' She points to the Dalma mountain range in the distance.

I can't stop the memories from taking over. 'How is Daadu? Does he still play the flute? We used to get drunk at his dhaba. And his wife made such delicious jalebis.'

'Niranjan runs the dhaba now; Daadu and Didima just supervise. During exam time, we can get cigarettes, coffee and sandwiches delivered to the hostel.'

I sit down on the steps of the auditorium and Cauvita settles down next to me. She's an attractive young woman. I light a cigarette and blow a smoke ring, which allows me to look at her without her knowledge.

'Are you from Jampot?'

'I worked for three years after engineering and then I

decided to take up HR. I wanted to dispel the myth that engineers can't do touchy-feely stuff.'

'If you are looking for someone who is good at that, your search stops here!' I smile at Cauvita, and she looks at me and giggles.

'Are you looking forward to meeting your old classmates?'

'Yes and no. Largely no, at this moment. It's so predictable, you know. After the first five minutes of bonhomie everyone gets down to competing with each other all over again. That's what I hate.'

'But you had such cool dudes in your batch. Alpana Rao was here last month to screen her latest film, *Dark Knights*. It won her an award in France. I believe she is making her next movie with Shahrukh Khan.'

'Yeah, not everyone ended up in the corporate world like me. Arunesh Nanda – you know, the rock guitarist – is also from the batch of '84,' I say with unmistakable pride.

'That's meant to be the surprise of this evening. He is performing the songs from his latest album, *Mood Swings*. My friend from Bombay says she often sees him in Bandra. I believe he lives somewhere there. What was he like when he was here?'

'He was always an amazing guitarist. His long hair made him look like a rock star even then. I remember when he played Dylan, especially "Blowing in the Wind" – anyone would have said he gave Bob a run for his money. That's according to Haathi. I believe he's heard Dylan live, so he knows. Arre, you should hear him do Kishore Kumar. He is just amazing. I saw his photo in *Stardust* the other day. The fucker now wears an earring and that, too, in one ear.'

'So which company did you join after leaving MIJ?'

'Balwanpur Industries. I just wanted to be in Delhi, and those buggers were the only ones to offer me a job in a place that was close. After that I think I got lazy and never changed jobs. I loved being in the factory. And life in that township is amazing.'

'The idea of living in a township is so romantic. I would love it.'

'Come over and spend a weekend with me.'

'Are you serious? I might take you up on it.'

'Promise.' I held out my hand and Cauvita put her rather cold hand in mine.

'Maybe I should use this alumni meeting to ask if any of them wants to hire someone like me. I am available to be employed by the highest bidder.'

The moon is playing hide and seek in the clouds. I can hear someone checking the PA system.

'1,2,3, mike testing hello... hello... mike testing...'

'Who the hell is this Mike who goes around testing sound systems?' I joke.

'Is it true that the first ten years of work are the most eventful in anyone's life?' Cauvita's question takes me by surprise.

Mine certainly were. When I joined MIJ in 1982, I thought that Delhi University had prepared me for everything I needed to know. When I joined Balwanpur Industries on 1 June 1984, I thought MIJ had taught me all the skiils required to navigate corporate India and life in general. I was bloody wrong.

# TWO

It is tough to start one's career at the bottom of the food chain. But that seemed to be the pattern of my life. Just as I learnt to claw my way to the top, life would reshuffle its cards and send me back to the bottom, and I would have to start all over again. So, when I became the cultural secretary of the students' union of my college, I thought I had finally cracked it. My good friend Kapil Aggarwal was the president of the SRCC Students' Union. Kapil and I agreed that we had achieved success in abundance. It was no mean achievement to be able to organize a rock concert along with Jai Mata College. Gosh, that girl Jas was cute. I was in love with her for almost two weeks before I got dumped. Naah... change that. It was MY decision to not pursue the relationship with Jas. It was taking too much time to start with. And I was a man in a hurry.

Kapil, of course, was secretly pleased with the outcome. He wanted me to be in love with Priya. I had explained to him a million times that it did not work well for my image to be seen to be in love with Priya who was not exactly the coolest or the prettiest chick in the University. But Kapil lived in a black and white world where one had the moral responsibility to propose to any girl one had spent more than five minutes talking to. He even called Priya 'bhabhi'.

'I am not going to go around with Priya just because you call her bhabhi.'

'I know she likes you, Abbey. And believe me, after marriage you will fall in love with her. In our culture, marriage comes before love. Whenever you want to come back to Priya, she will be waiting at the doorstep for you.'

I have to admit that it was Priya and Kapil who filled in my admission form for MIJ and they were the ones most happy for me when I got in. Ironically, MIJ was the reason I grew more and more distant from both of them.

I started at the bottom of the totem pole when I joined MIJ for an MBA in Personnel Management. (Yeah, I KNOW these days it's called Human Resources Management.) It was Rustom Topiwalla, my new and wise-beyond-his-years classmate, who taught me that the shortest distance between two points was not always ethical but it did get you better grades. And finally, after too many years of feeling hopelessly inadequate, I managed a job with Balwanpur Industries as their Personnel Executive.

My mind went back to that day when I left the campus in the summer of 1984 and boarded the train from

Tatanagar station for Delhi. Jamshedpur was called 'Jampot' for a reason: the students took over the city for two years and became an integral part of it, even if they only returned once or twice, for an alumni meet.

The same Tatanagar Express that had brought us to Jampot in 1982 was now taking us away from it two years later. We were all sitting there clutching our degrees and a swirl of memories of the two years just past. I was part of the 'Delhi gang' along with Joy, Pappu, Funny, Arunesh, Gur and Neetika. Even that disgusting slob Gopher was going to Delhi. He had got a job there and was 'joining them immediately to build maximum seniority in the company'. Ayesha was as usual the star attraction in our compartment, dressed in her tight jeans and an even tighter green T-shirt that said 'Only a Rat Wins the Rat Race'. She was used to being the cynosure of all eyes at MIJ and loved it. She was sitting next to me now and reading *Stardust* which had a special story on Amitabh Bachchan. I was conscious of her shoulder rubbing against mine as the train chugged along. It felt good.

'Abbey, listen to this. Last year Amitabh Bachchan burnt his left hand during Diwali. So during the shooting of *Sharaabi,* he had to keep his hand in his pocket. That became the trademark of his character.'

'Hmm...'

'Amitabh's voice is such a turn on, isn't it?'

'Hmm...'

'Missing MIJ?'

'Hmm...'

'Missing Keya, aren't you, Abbey?'

'Yeah. I wonder what she wanted to tell me back there, at the station. I wish I'd had a chance to talk to her before I left Jampot for good.'

'I know you still love her.'

Ayesha looked up from her magazine, waiting for my response.

I said quietly, 'Ayesha, how does one stop loving someone?'

My relationship with Keya may have come to an abrupt end but I preferred to think of it as an inflexion point from which it would evolve over time. The spark had continued to grow somewhere within and silently consume me over the past year. I would often talk about it to Pappu, my roommate for the first year at MIJ, who had seen my feelings for Keya develop from the day when I first came back from play rehearsal, completely smitten by her. He had seen me wait outside the BEd college on campus for Keya's classes to end so that we could go for a walk or spend an afternoon together in the empty auditorium, the only place where we could get enough privacy for the things we needed to do.

The day after I came back to Jampot for my second year at MIJ, Keya had asked me what my 'plans' were. I explained my career aspirations with a precision that would have made any employer offer me a job. Keya just walked away. I didn't even get a chance to ask her what

I had done wrong. And every time I tried to make sense of what had happened, only one thing came to mind: that slimeball Gopher must have tattled to her about the night I spent in Ayesha's flat on the last day of our summer training in Bombay. That must have done it.

I looked at Gopher shelling peanuts with the concentration of a monkey and littering the floor with the clumsiness of one. He was lost in thought. I saw Ayesha looking at me, wondering why I had not completed the answer to her question.

'It must have something to do with my inability to complete anything. When a toothpaste tube has the last few days' worth of paste left in it, I start using a new tube. The previous one's status is left undecided: it's neither over nor is it active. Maybe my relationship with Keya is a bit like that.'

'Abbey, that is disgusting. To think of a relationship like a toothpaste.'

'I didn't mean it like that! What I meant was, I find it hard to bring closure to things. I would rather leave them open-ended.'

Joy had opened a bottle of Old Monk and Pappu had got Gur and Funny to open up bottles of Thums Up. Neetika alias Neats pulled out a huge packet of peanuts. Gopher immediately tucked away his own packet under his pillow and started digging into the community resources. Arunesh Nanda had an eager audience. We took a swig of the familiar Old Monk-Thums Up concoction (OM-TU or OM2, as the junior batch at MIJ called it).

Arunesh strummed a few chords and said, 'I learnt this song in my previous life before I came to MIJ. For the benefit of Gopher, let me translate the lyrics. The guy is telling his girlfriend that she should stay in his heart and not pay a paisa as rent. And then adds that she should make a mattress out of his dreams and in the morning while she washes her face with Pears soap, he will shed a steady supply of tears so that she doesn't need tap water.'

Mere dil ka quarter kar le occupy
Mat dena darling rent ka single pai

Mere sapnon ki bed pe darling sona
Subah uthho toh Pears sabun se mukhda dhona
Main karunga, main karunga,
Main karunga apne ankhon se water supply
Mat dena darling rent ka single pai

Gopher completed the destruction of the song with his nasal response.

'Sounds like a good idea to save on rent, da. In Delhi I'll have to spend so much money on house rent.'

I lit a cigarette and took a sip of OM2. We continued drinking and singing for the better part of the journey. Gur and Neetika continued to coochie-coo like newly-weds. Pappu gulped down his drinks and then did what he did best. He slept. We knew he would have to be yanked out of slumber at the railway station in Delhi.

Ayesha had fallen asleep too, with my shoulder for a pillow. Her thick hair shielded her face from view. I thought for a moment about waking her, then decided to let her sleep undisturbed.

# THREE

The day I landed with an MBA degree from MIJ, I sensed new respect for me at home. Everyone just seemed to know that I had arrived. Even my kid sister Asmita (lovingly called Ass for short) wanted career advice from me. My parents were very obviously proud of their son's achievement and made their feelings known to all those who visited us. I basked in the glory of a freshly made MBA.

The moment I got home, bag and baggage, my mother took one look at me and said, 'Ishshsh! Look how thin Chotka has become.'

She was the only one who saw me as a 'thin' scrawny child. The rest of the world thought I looked exceptionally well-fed. My father and sister were part of the rest of the world team.

'Rubbish! He looks just fine. Ask him to start doing free hand exercises every morning. It will prepare him better for hard labour when he starts his career. There is not much time left. If you don't work out his routine on day one, he will spend the whole month just eating and sleeping. These days every second loafer on the streets has a degree in management. He will have to work very hard.'

'Chotka needs to first look after himself. These two years in the hostel have destroyed his health. He must have had to work through the day without thinking of food or sleep. We have only thirty days to put his health back on track.' Ma knew what to focus on.

'Bhai, what are you planning to study next? Baba was suggesting that you sign up for another degree,' Ass suggested, and made a face at me as she stepped behind Dad – out of my reach. But the damage was done.

'Khukumoni, you have a sharp memory. Good you reminded me of that.' Dad was the only one who continued calling her by the generic name given to all Bengali girls until their official name is agreed upon.

I made a mental note to yank Asmita's pigtails once Baba was out of sight. When I left MIJ, I had made a promise to myself that I would never EVER read anything again. I was done with my share of time in classrooms and grovelling before profs to hike up my grade from C to a respectable B. I could not handle one more day of that. However, management theory had taught me that no long-term plan had any meaning until the immediate problem had been sorted out. I remembered Father Hathaway's much quoted line: 'Problems cannot be solved. They can be absolved, resolved or dissolved.'

I tried to distract everyone by asking for change to pay the taxi driver. The ploy worked and I bought myself some breathing time.

The 'in between time' as Ayesha liked to call it, was a perfect blend of joy and lack of responsibility. It was a lot like the three years I'd spent floating aimlessly in Delhi University. The only difference was that now I had the three magical alphabets M-B-A attached to my name.

First, I had to catch up with Kapil and Priya. I promised to meet Kapil at Connaught Place.

He looked rather more grown up than I remembered, in his white kurta pajama and shades. He was chewing paan in the most disgusting way possible. And yet I was thrilled to see him.

I hugged him and said, 'Kapil! You look like a mafia don with those dark glasses. All that's missing is a gold chain.'

He missed the sarcasm completely. 'I will have a gold chain, yaar. I am saving money for it. Give me another year. How do you like my new scooter?'

Kapil drove me to his house in Chandni Chowk on his new two-wheeler. I saw the historic Red Fort to my right and knew we would soon be in the narrow lanes and by-lanes of Chandni Chowk. One after the other, we would go past all the places of worship, starting with the Jain temple on the left, the Hindu temple and church on either side of the street, past Gurdwara Sees Ganj and finally the Jama Masjid. Kapil stopped at the jalebi shop where we both had piping hot jalebis dripping sugar syrup. He parked the scooter in the lane and invited me to walk up the narrow steps that led to his place on the first floor. They were so steep, it was like climbing a ladder. I stubbed out my cigarette before I entered Kapil's house.

'I have to give you some bad news about Priya bhabhi,' said Kapil.

'Let me guess. She is actually going to sing a song when we meet,' I joked.

'No, that kutta fellow she was to get married to...'

'Yeah, that silly sod Neel, who promised to give her a break in Bollywood. I always knew he was lying – he doesn't know R.D. Burman or anybody else for that matter. He's just a small-time crook trying to make money. She is an ass for believing that Neel is her well-wisher. I saw the wedding invite. It was crass and reeked of poor taste.'

'Abbey, that kutta boy Neelu finally did not come for the shaadi. Imagine yaar, it was so bad that she went into depressun after that. Even I had tears in my eyes looking at her condisun.'

'WHAT? You mean Neel never showed up for the wedding? What a dog! So what is Priya up to now? I hope she hasn't stopped singing?'

'No, I haven't,' said Priya as she stepped out of Kapil's room.

I was not prepared for this. Priya looked just the same. She wore a red and yellow salwar kurta and her hair was only a little longer than I remembered. I noticed that she had contacts on, not the usual thick glasses. In the past, whenever Priya hugged me, I would wince and wait for the awkward moment to pass. This time I hugged her back.

'I am so happy to see you, Priya. I am so sorry that… Actually I didn't know that you didn't finally… you know…'

'I don't blame you, Abbey. Usually when you receive an invitation card for a wedding, you assume that the wedding would have taken place. How were you to know?'

'That bastard Neel… I knew he was good for nothing. That bloody cheat…'

Priya hugged me closer. 'It happens to everyone, Abbey. We all go through difficult times. But it's at times like this you realize how lucky you are to have friends. Kapil stood by me like a rock. And I knew that I could always reach out to you. It doesn't hurt any more, you know. Though it did, then.'

I knew Priya was trying hard to be brave. I looked away to give her space to blink away the hurt.

We were interrupted by Kapil suddenly clearing his throat very loudly to announce that lunch had been served. I was still trying to come to terms with what I'd just heard. I couldn't even begin to imagine what Priya must have gone through when Neel abandoned her at the mandap. What a bastard.

Over lunch, Priya told me that she was working on recording nursery rhymes in Hindi. Her next project was to re-record some children's songs from old Hindi films.

'The first song should be "Nanha munna rahi hoon" from *Son of India*,' I suggested.

'So it shall be. You always come up with such perfect suggestions. Quiz question for you, Abbey. Who sang that song?'

'Shanti Mathur. I know that one.'

'Ten points to Team A,' said Priya, miming like she was on TV.

Kapil kept his eyes on the parathas. His mother insisted that we eat more. I looked at my watch and realized I was never going to make it in time to meet Ayesha at CP. I was to meet her at 3 p.m. Kapil suggested that we go together, in an autorickshaw.

'I have to meet a classmate from MIJ who is looking to rent a room. Her office is going to be in CP, so she wants to live around there. But she's new to the city, so I thought I'd help,' I explained to Kapil and Priya as we set off.

Priya could always find something nice to say. 'You are such a thoughtful person, Abbey. It makes such a difference to be in an unfamiliar city with a friend. When I went to Simla for the first time with Neel...'

'Bhabhi, why you are talking of him? That book is closed.'

'You mean it's a closed chapter, right. Priya, that bastard Neel deserves to be electrocuted for what he did to you.' I was really angry.

'Abbey, there's no point in being so angry. I know you hate Neel, but I can't help feeling he gave me a chance to pursue my dreams. I was really happy during those two years, you know. It was my fault that I pushed him into marrying me. He wasn't emotionally prepared for it. Everyone tries to do the best they can in life. Neel did, too.'

Then Kapil did one of the dumbest things ever done by a human being. He leaned over, nudged me and asked in a stage whisper, 'Abbey, why don't you marry Priya bhabhi? I know you are both loving each other.'

'Of course not. Why should I be the one to marry Priya?' I blurted. Which made it sound like a punishment, of course!

'Kapil, I need to get back to your house. I left my handbag on your study table. Please ask him to stop the auto, I need to get off. Bhaiya, zara gaadi rokna.'

Kapil and Priya got out and walked away and I was left sitting in the auto, feeling stupid.

*Why did you say it that way, Abbey?*

*I don't know. It was not meant to hurt Priya. I really was happy to see both of them. I really was. Kapil ruined it all with that daft question.*

*Abbey, you are talking to yourself. Can you please be honest? You know exactly who ruined what and for whom.*

*I value her as a friend. She has always beeen there to console me every time some girl gave me the cold shoulder – which was often.*

*Yeah right, she was always there for you. But today, when you found out what she's been through, did you reach out to her?*

I sat in the auto, lost in thought. I knew without doubt that Priya loved me unconditionally. Yet, I would cringe each time I had to attend a college festival with her for company. She was so not cool – the way she dressed, hung on to me like Band Aid and worst of all, agreed vehemently with everything I said or did. I had once told her to get a mind of her own and not lease mine all the time. She had just looked at me adoringly and said it always surprised her how clever I was. It was like Father Hathaway used to say: 'I don't get what I want. And I don't want what I get.'

I saw Ayesha standing near Regal cinema. She was wearing a tight pair of Levis and a white T-shirt with Tibetan art on it. Her hair looked a faint shade of brown and her shades (I used to refer to them as 'goggles' until she set me right) concealed her eyes.

'Abbey, I just love the buzz of this place. Let's go have coffee somewhere.'

'Aren't we supposed to check out some options for you to stay?'

'We certainly could check this place out.' Ayesha flashed a set of keys. 'This guy lives in the US and has an apartment on Park Avenue in Manhattan. He bought this beautifully furnished apartment in the heart of CP and is willing to let me live there. It's a perfect arrangement. He comes to India for a week in a year. I just need to find a place to stay for that week. Maybe I could stay with you? What do you say?'

I nodded. I had no idea how I could get Ayesha to live with me for a week, discreetly. It would be impossible. I thought of Baba's reaction to the idea of Ayesha staying with me and then shook off the thought. But I made a mental note to think up a solution soon.

We took a rick to the apartment that Ayesha had the

keys to, and it was like we'd walked into a fancy five-star hotel. This was an apartment the likes of which I had only seen in film magazines. Obviously, Ayesha had struck gold.

'What's the rent like? Must be totally unaffordable.'

Ayesha responded by walking up to me and unbuttoning my shirt.

She looked at me and murmured, 'There's electricity between us, Abbey. Don't you feel it too?'

And I came up with my corniest yet: 'I've got the perfect lightning rod for you.'

And so we inaugurated the apartment. Over the next few days Ayesha and I revelled in the freedom of having a room to ourselves. There was no need to hurry or sneak around. We were both planning to start work from the first of June, so a whole month lay ahead in which to perfect our routine.

# FOUR

'No matter where you are, make sure you are home at 8 p.m. for dinner.'

Baba had laid down this rule many moons ago and it could not be challenged. So at about 7 p.m. I would have to leave off whatever we were doing and announce to Ayesha that I needed to get going.

I would rush home to be greeted by Asmita at the door. She would ask loudly and innocently, 'What's the time, Baba?' The trick never failed to work. Baba would glare at his watch and my face in turn.

'It is 8:06 p.m. You are late as usual. You should be utilizing these last few weeks to cultivate a disciplined approach to life. But you wake up late and then spend the whole day doing God knows what.'

'Chotka is now an MBA. He has to keep track of so many things. He was telling me that reading one newspaper is not enough. He goes to a library in CP to read the *Economic Times*. Will you please let him eat in peace now?' Ma was always ready to bail me out.

'Did you read the news about your new company?'

I looked at him blankly.

'Something about the possibility of it going public. It was on the third page of the *Hindustan Times*. What do you know about it?'

Baba was clearly trying to learn about this mysterious thing called the Private Sector – something he viewed with a combination of awe and disgust for its flashy ways.

I repeated whatever I could remember from the pre-placement talk at the campus: 'Balwanpur Paper was set up in 1964 by Rai Bahadur Sangram Singh as a gift for his grandson Balwan Singh. The paper company soon diversified into chemicals and oils and was renamed Balwanpur Industries. I am going to be on the rolls of Balwanpur Paper as that is the holding company. Balwanpur Industries employs close to 5000 people among all its divisions. They run the entire township of Balwanpur. I will have to live there as well.'

On most days, I'm proof that Isaac Newton was a genius. After all, it was he who had discovered that a body at rest will continue to be at rest – until he is yanked out of bed. On D-Day, however, it was different.

I woke up on 1 June 1984 with a feeling of excitement tempered with uncertainty. It was going to be the first day of my work life. What was in store for me in the days and years to come?

I pulled out the letter that I had received from the company the week before. It was typed neatly on the letterhead of Balwanpur Industries. I felt a strange sense of pride as I read the letter. It proved to me that no matter how pathetic my grades, having an MBA from MIJ meant the corporate world was ready to take a chance on me.

> Dear Sir,
>
> With reference to our discussions we are pleased to invite you to join the management team at Balwanpur Industries as Personnel Executive.
>
> Please report to the bus stop on Parliament Street at 9:30 a.m. on 1 June 1984. The office car will take you from there to the factory at Balwanpur. You will be assigned a fully furnished room…

The rest of the letter was full of administrivia but it had been signed by the Chairman and Managing Director, Mr Singh himself.

I was up now and dressed in a crisp starched blue shirt and black trousers. My shoes were polished and shining. Ma had put together an elaborate breakfast and bade me farewell with teary eyes as she watched me put my suitcases into the cab. Asmita gave me a hug that also allowed her to discreetly wipe her tears.

Baba stood by, stoically preparing to send me off to the battlefield. He put his hands on my head as I bent down to touch his feet.

'Remember what the *Bhagwad Gita* says. Do your best and do not worry about the results. Never cut corners. Your boss must always rely on you for everything. In the private sector, it is very important to keep the boss happy. Otherwise you could be summarily dismissed.'

As I touched Ma's feet she turned to Baba and said in a voice choked with emotion, 'Why must you be so insensitive and say such things just when Chotka is about to start on his journey? Wait, now I must give him some doi-mishti one more time.'

Asmita was dispatched to get some sandesh and sweet yogurt that Ma managed to organize whenever we had visitors from Calcutta. Ma's good luck charms were always food-centric! Baba did not risk saying anything the second time round, for fear of delaying me.

At 9.30, as promised, a white Ambassador marked with a Balwanpur Industries sticker drew up at the bus stop near Jantar Mantar, and I was off.

When we got to the township of Balwanpur, five hours later, I was dropped off at the apartment block that was to be my new 'home'. It reminded me of the professors' quarters at MIJ, except that these had two apartments, not four, to a block. My apartment had the luxury of a small garden since I was on the ground floor. As I opened the gate and walked in, a pesky little dog appeared on the lawn and proceeded to water the flowers. Then it shut its eyes and relieved itself right in the middle of the green. I like dogs for the most part, what annoyed me was the blissful look on its face as it closed its eyes and let go in three equal instalments.

A shrill feminine voice sounded from the balcony of the apartment on the first floor: 'Funtoosh! Come back. Right now. Don't make Mama angry, beta.'

The dachshund responded by swiftly digging up my

lawn to cover up the evidence before running up the stairs. I followed suit – I mean, I too walked up the stairs. 'Devi Dayal', said the nameplate on the door.

I wasn't sure I wanted to pick a fight on day one. I debated for a moment whether I should get aggressive or discuss the matter amiably. Or perhaps I could indulge in guerilla warfare and get myself a dog that would do the needful at Devi Dayal's doorstep.

'Please come in. I am Mrs Dayal. I was just coming to invite you over for lunch.' I looked at the plump matronly lady draped in a garish purple saree. Her lips were painted a dark, exaggerated red.

'No, I just wanted to say hello.' I decided not to bring up Funtoosh's bowel movements as the opening move. I noticed the dog squinting at me as it furiously wagged its tail against the curtain. 'I have to go to the office right now. Maybe I will drop in for dinner some day. Thanks.'

At the personnel department, I was made to fill out a million forms and shake many hands before I was sent to meet the Medical Officer, Dr Patronobish, for a medical examination. He ordered me to strip and spent more time examining my equipment than any other part of my body before declaring me fit to join duty. And all through, he talked.

'Hi, I am Doctor Patronobish. Better known as Pat. When I went to the UK on a fellowship, my colleagues found my last name a bit of a tongue-twister. So they shortened it to a manageable Pat. You know, this is the first time Balwanpur Industries has hired an MBA. You must meet the CMD, Balwan Singhji. I heard that he signed your appointment letter himself. Normally he signs only the General Manager's appointment letter. By the way, your boss Captain Sobti is known in Balwanpur as the Grandmaster – he is a survivor, the master puppeteer of Balwanpur Industries. You have to be in his good books if you are thinking of a career in this company.

'Come home for a drink someday when you've settled in. My house is in the Senior Managers' Complex. Sobti himself sanctioned it. After all, he owes his life to me.'

'You saved his life?' I asked.

'He was driving back to Balwanpur after meeting Balwan Singhji in Delhi. It was raining and at night that road can be a difficult one to drive on. On the way the car was stopped by six masked people – possibly workers from the factory. Sobti was slightly drunk and so his reflexes were dull. Those guys hammered him with rods and chains until they thought he was dead. I happened to be driving back from the workers' quarters. I recognized Sobti lying there in a pool of blood and rushed him to the hospital in the nick of time. Your boss is a controversial character, you see, and sometimes that goes against him.'

Armed with Dr Patronobish's clearance I went to meet the Grandmaster. He had not yet returned from lunch. So I waited in his room and looked at the office done up entirely in expensive looking teak, with curios from various parts of India. I spotted a shawl from the northeast. There was a spear and an oversized Nepalese kukri that seemed sharp enough to behead any man or beast. The room smelt of cigars. I wondered if there was some liquor stashed away in the locked wooden cabinet. Or perhaps it contained confidential files?

'Hi, Abbey. Welcome to Balwanpur Industries. I am Captain Sobti. Call me Captain. And stop fiddling with your pen. There's no need to be so nervous. Your shirt is all creased and that tells me you've come from Pat's clinic. The buckle of your belt is off-centre too. Pat must have asked you to take off your pants. He likes to check if you have the balls necessary to be in my department.' He guffawed like a maniac.

I was standing right next to the door. How had I missed seeing him walk in? Sobti must have read my mind.

'There are six doors that lead into my office. The visitors all use the one you came through. I use the others. The mirrors on the ceiling helped me to take a good look at you before you even reacted to my presence. Personnel management is all about knowing people. I haven't been to a fancy business school like you, so I have to use my sense of observation.'

I looked up at the ceiling that was entirely covered with mirrors. Sobti was over six feet tall and had a prominent moustache that had been carefully trimmed and shaped. He wore tight clothes that showed off his muscular body. A small leather bag with brass clips was slung across his chest. His eyes were piercing, they made you feel as though he was reading your mind. He pulled out a cigar and lit it.

'These cigars have been rolled by Burmese women on their thighs. Do you smoke? Try one.'

I should have said no. Instead, I inhaled deeply, only to experience a near collapse. I choked. I coughed loudly and rolled up my eyes. It took a full minute for the world to right itself.

'So the thought of the women's thighs made you try stuff you otherwise wouldn't. Remember, your colleagues must never know what makes you salivate. The day they find out, you are history. Your career will always be dependent on staying clear of temptation.'

I nodded. He continued, 'Most people believe that the reason they feel confident enough to join personnel management is that they get along with other people and therefore they would enjoy working with people. The more important question is: do people enjoy spending time with you? Do they see you as their trusted advisor? I always tell them that's a question they need to ask themselves on the day they retire. It is a tough profession to be in. You have to be close to people and yet be distant enough to retain the ability to take hard decisions about them. That's not easy, my friend. It's not easy even after so many years.'

I looked at Captain Sobti's eyes. They sparkled when he spoke.

'You have made a smart career move by starting your professional life in the factory. There is no substitute for learning people management skills by trying out your theories on the shopfloor. That is where you will learn how the business really works and how to work with people to make work happen.'

I nodded in agreement. I couldn't exactly tell him that I would have much preferred life in the corporate office with the bigwigs rather than a factory with its attendant sweat and grime.

'You are already the subject of much speculation in this company, Abbey. And when the old man – yeah, that's what I call the CMD – invites you to play golf, the rest of the company gets ready to stab you, first chance they get. But don't shy away from the opportunity. Be respectful while talking to him, but don't hesitate to give him your own opinion. There are enough people who act like his echo-chamber.'

He pulled out a card. 'Here's the invitation to join him at his personal golf course at 5:30 a.m.'

I wiped the sweat off my brow and bleated, 'I don't know how to play golf, Captain.'

'You have until tomorrow morning to learn. Remember, I want you there at 5:30 sharp.'

I went back to my apartment and found Mrs Dayal waiting for me to have dinner. I mumbled something about having a headache and promised to join her over the weekend. She insisted on sending dinner across. I was so annoyed at this imposition that I promptly threw the food into the garbage bin.

I called Ayesha. She had had a great day. She told me what a lovely office she had.

'You know the office is on Janpath. The boss and I

decided to go out for lunch. Then we stopped for coffee and I just got back. He is a really smart guy and I think he likes me already. He has given me a cabin right next to his. I can make long-distance calls from his phone. You don't need to call me and spend money, Abbey. I'll call you from my office phone.'

'Listen, the CMD wants me to play golf with him. What do I do?'

'So play golf! What's the problem, Abbey? I've got to go now. Bye.'

I couldn't believe Ayesha could be so self-centred. She didn't care about my problems. And it annoyed me that she was flirting with her boss. I lit a cigarette and blew smoke rings at the ceiling. Then I went to the cupboard and pulled out a bottle of Old Monk that Ayesha had given me.

'The only one for the lonely one,' Ayesha had said with a wicked smile as she handed me the bottle.

When I reached the golf course the next morning, it was 5:29 a.m. I saw two men carrying golf clubs, and striding ahead of them, the smartly attired figure of Balwan Singh. I walked up to him and introduced myself.

'So, he is the MBA we have recruited from MIJ,' said Balwan Singh to no one in particular as he hit the golf ball and sent it away to hell and beyond.

He was a short stocky man in his forties. He wore a T-shirt that showed off his beer belly and a golf cap that probably covered his bald patch. On his wrist was a gold watch that glistened as it caught the rays of the sun.

*Nobody actually wears a watch made of gold, stupid. It must be gold coloured.*

*But he is the CMD. He must be filthy rich. He employs 5000 people, that's how rich he is. That watch is made of gold.*

Balwan Singh spoke to me while practising his swing two inches away from the ball. Golf was clearly his passion.

'Do you play golf? I bet you do. No one chooses a career in the private sector without knowing the career opportunities this beautiful game has to offer. You should spend your mornings here on the greens. It will be good for your health and wealth,' Balwan Singh said, and whipped the ball sharply. I nodded in agreement.

'I am just a beginner. I can't play against you, at least not yet.'

'You don't play golf AGAINST anyone. That is the beauty of this game. You play it against yourself and against the forces of nature. No two shots are ever identical, because everything changes from moment to moment – from the direction of the wind to the temperature, and your own mood. Each moment is a snapshot of life itself.'

Just then, Captain Sobti turned up. He shook hands with Balwan Singh and said, 'Abhinav joined us yesterday. I'll take him around now, to meet the union leaders. I asked him to meet me here so that I could take him with me. Great shot!'

'Captain! You always know how to pick the best. I

hope you'll enjoy working with us, young man. Why don't you stop by my office at 3 p.m. this afternoon?'

I followed Sobti as he briskly walked through the golf course and towards the office building, trying to keep pace.

'I'm glad I didn't have to play golf with the boss, Captain. I was born without a single sporting gene in my body.'

Sobti's response took me by surprise. 'You only spoke to the CMD. What about the two people with him? You ignored them.' He barely glanced at me as he spoke.

'But they weren't officers. They looked like his caddies, or maybe peons…'

'The way you treat people who don't matter shows your real character. Never ignore those who cannot do anything for you, except of course pray for you. Remember, sometimes prayers work better than strategies in the corporate world.'

# FIVE

Balwanpur was a world in itself. Everyone knew everyone. But there were clear boundaries marked out for each group. The factory workers lived in the Workers' Housing Complex where each building had identically designed two-room houses with a small patch of green allotted to every house. The road went through the busy complex like veins running through the body. Right in the middle was a small market where farmers from the neighbouring villages came to sell vegetables and meat.

There was also a more upmarket shopping complex where the officers and managers could shop. The greatest attraction here was an ice cream parlour called Happy to Talk. It was the only shop that was 'allowed to sell' ice cream, cakes and coffee – essential items for anybody who wished to be seen as upwardly mobile. The other chief attraction was the colour television that telecast the latest Bollywood hits. The owner's son Happy Singh was the playboy of the town. Apparently, Happy Singh had almost got shot by his father when he gave up his turban in favour of short hair and the 'imported T-shirt' look. All over the store were posters of the sauciest Bollywood starlets, more perhaps for the young man's viewing pleasure than for the customers.

Then there was the Officers' Housing Complex where I lived. These were small, fully furnished two-room apartments. On the second day after I moved in, someone had stopped by and made me sign on a list of items that had been provided in my apartment. It was an exhaustive list. I knew now that there were eighteen light points in my flat. And that I had been allotted '1 no. dining table with four chairs (no cushions)'. There was also, wonder of wonders, a small Kelvinator refrigerator, which employees in my grade were not entitled to. 'Management's discretion', I gathered. I was soon the subject of conversation in the township. Opinion was sharply divided as to the appropriateness of a personnel executive being given a fridge. Mrs Devi Dayal came over and congratulated me.

'I am so happy that they have started treating officers at par with managers. Do you know that a fridge is something only deputy managers are entitled to?'

'I am certainly very happy to be given a fridge. Now I can get chilled beer right through the year.'

'And I can come over to get ice whenever I want.'

The Senior Managers' Complex had twenty-five houses, each with four bedrooms. The furniture was better, the bathroom fittings were snazzier. How did I know that? I got invited by Captain Sobti to his house one evening. A few drinks down, when I tottered across to the bathroom down the hallway, I couldn't help but notice the lavish lifestyle my boss had. The bedroom and the drawing room were equipped with air-conditioners. That was proof that he was really high up in the pecking order.

I learnt from Mrs Dayal that the company paid the electricity bills for the managers.

'So what do they do for the four directors? Do they pay for their own toilet paper or is that part of the perks?' I asked her one day.

'For them, everything, and I mean everything, is paid for by the company. Each of them has four cooks – one to cook Indian food, one to cook Continental food, one who specializes in desserts and one for snacks. Each cook has an assistant. They are called "choppers". Their job is to chop the vegetables and clean the kitchen after the cooks are done.'

'What are those houses like, I wonder?'

'Don't worry. You'll get there one day, I am sure. Already the company has given you a fridge. I heard that, at the Ladies' Club, they had a heated discussion about it. Since I am in the accounts department I get to know everything. All the bills come to me for clearance.'

'Wow. So you are a very important person. You clear the directors' claims?'

'No, that is done by my boss, N.S.R Ramadorai. He knows every rule ever made in this organization. He makes sure that no one gets a rupee more than the rules permit them to claim. I clear the managers' entertainment bills. Every month they have to entertain other employees or government officials. Those bills all come to me for reimbursement.' Mrs Dayal was obviously conscious of the power she wielded.

The next evening she came over and invited me home for dinner. She smiled mysteriously and said that she had invited some other guests too. I wasn't sure what the protocol was, so I chose to wear my favourite black shirt and blue jeans combination, doused myself with some aftershave and went for dinner. Already seated in the rather fussily done up drawing room were a middle-aged man and a young lady in her twenties.

'This is Mr Ramadorai, my boss. And this is his daughter Rajani.'

I shook hands with both father and daughter and realized that Ramadorai was not very pleased about my shaking his daughter's hand within the first three minutes of our meeting. But it was too late. I sat around and made polite conversation with them. The usual stuff about where I had grown up and which college I had gone to, what life was like at MIJ etc. It felt like a job interview, with Ramadorai asking all the questions and listening intently to my answers.

Mrs Dayal must have sensed my growing discomfort. She said that Rajani and I could check out her collection of books and music in the other room while she finished talking to Ramadorai about some office matters. I heaved a sigh of relief and walked into the guest room with its collection of books. Mostly Asimov and Ludlum novels, and a shelf full of Alistair Maclean. Rajani followed me silently. I hadn't heard her speak yet and wasn't sure how to initiate a dialogue. But once she was out of earshot of her father, she seemed to transform into a regular college girl.

'Was it tough to get admission to MIJ? I believe it's the toughest entrance exam to clear, is that right?' Rajani said.

'No and no.'

'What?'

'It isn't tough to get into MIJ because I got through, and since I got through, the entrance exams certainly can't be tough, or I wouldn't have cleared them.'

Rajani giggled and said, 'I did a BA from Stella Maris in Madras. That gave me a chance to run away from this boring town even if it was for a short while. I did everything that I couldn't have done if I had gone to college somewhere near Balwanpur. The weekends used to be wild. There was a group of us that used to paint the town red.'

Rajani Ramadorai hardly seemed like someone who would go about town with a can of red. Looks can be deceptive.

'Yeah, living in the hostel gave me a chance to explore my wild side too. We used to have this stuff called WCDMR – WC-Dimmer, which stood for Who Can Drink More Rum. I wanted so badly to win the DMR King title but never managed to. There was actually a time when one of the girls became a serious contestant. Do you mind if I smoke?'

'Not at all. I tried smoking a few times, but finally chose to give it up. So what were the girls like at MIJ?'

'They were pretty cool. Like any other college crowd, we had all kinds. Do you have a lot of parties here?'

'This town is not the place for parties. I mean, we do have parties, but they are rather formal and staid affairs. You can't expect the wild partying that you might have had at MIJ. Maybe you should organize one. I would love to help you organize a party.'

'So why did you give up the freedom you had in Madras and come back to this one-horse town?'

'I missed Daddy. I lost my mother when I was very young. And now that Appa is growing older... He is going to retire in a few years, unless Mr Singh gives him an extension. He wants to start his own financial consultancy firm to advise people on how to invest their money. He is pretty good at playing the stock market. He is so conservative that unless he is hundred per cent sure that a share will make money, he will not invest in it. He has never made a loss in the stock market,' Rajani said proudly.

Shortly afterwards, Mrs Dayal called us in for dinner. I focussed on the food. Ramadorai asked all sorts of personal questions, including at what age Asmita was planning to get married. It was with a sense of relief that I finally said goodnight and went back home.

The next morning Ramadorai sent me prasadam from what was supposedly the family temple. The day after, he sent me an old circular that informed me that if I got married while I was an employee of Balwanpur Industries, I would be eligible to choose between 'a crockery set and a VIP suitcase'. He recommended over the telephone that I choose the suitcase because the crockery set was not of good quality and most people who had got married had complained, he said.

'Complained about getting married?' I asked.

'No, complained about the quality of the crockery. What is your date of birth?' he asked matter-of-factly.

'16 November.'

'What about the year and place of birth?'

'Will it qualify me for extra privileges and perks?' I asked before answering him and hanging up.

There was the rest of the Balwanpur township and then there was the Mansion. The golf course was garlanded by an artificial lake called Sangram Sarovar. In the middle of the green was the CMD's house. One part of it was used by Balwan Singh to entertain his employees. Government officials were entertained in yet another part. Diwan-e-Aam and Diwan-e-Khaas, as the office gossip put it. I couldn't wait to be invited.

'Be careful what you wish for, Abbey. It may come true,' said Captain Sobti.

I showed him my newly printed business cards and said, 'Look at my visiting card. It tells the whole world that I am a personnel executive – there's a very long way to go.'

'Isn't it strange how the visiting card seems to define a person's identity? The way someone introduces himself tells you how he sees himself. Some people introduce themselves by their first name – these are the ones who like to shape their own destiny.'

'Well then, I know exactly how I want to introduce myself – as a manager in this company, like you, with a house in the Managers' Colony. It seems a bit pointless to me, not being called a manager even after getting a degree in management.'

'A consultant once taught me that you can put most things in life into a 2x2 matrix. Let's take this very instance. In life you can be a big fish or a small fish. The pond you swim in can be either big or small. When you put this in a 2x2 matrix, you discover that right now you are a small fish with a strong desire to become big. Balwanpur is a pond. You can decide whether this pond is big or small. For the moment it seems like a big pond to you since you chose this job while still in college. That makes you a small fish in a small pond.

'The next stage will be for you to become a big fish in the small pond. That's when professional credibility is built. This is the most difficult stage and most people give up the game when they encounter the first signs of resistance. To be a big fish, you have to learn to demonstrate comfort while handling all the other small fish. Patience is the name of the game.

'You still have a long way to go, Abbey. First build your rapport with the workers. Go visit them. Get to know them and their families, their problems, their social issues and their dreams. Try to be a big fish in a small pond.'

'People here tell me that you know each of the 5000 workers and their families on a first-name basis. Is that true?'

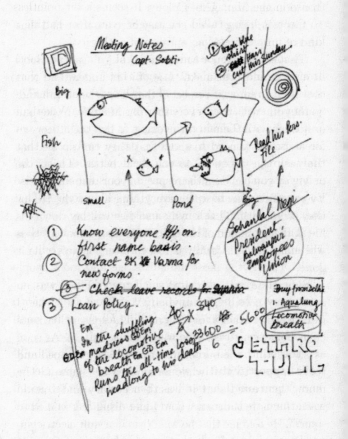

Meeting Notes:
Capt. Sobti

① Wash blue shirt
② Get hair cut this Sunday

Big

Fish

Small          Pond

Read his kes. File

Sohanlal Negi
President,
balwarpur
Employees
Union

① Know everyone fff on first name basis
② Contact SK Varma for new forms
③ Check leave records for Sharma
③ Loan Policy.

Em
In the shuffling madness
of the locomotive breath
Runs the all-time loser
headlong to his death

40 × $40
48 = $600
33600
6

Buy from Delhi
1. Aqualung
Locomotive breath

JETHRO TULL

'Perhaps not all the family members. My training in the Army comes in handy. There is a lot to learn from that organization, Abbey.'

'Captain, things would be easy here too if we had that kind of unquestioned acceptance of authority.'

'That's where you are mistaken, Abbey.' Captain Sobti lit a cigar and continued, 'The officers understand that they need to earn the respect of the troops they command. So they run with them every morning and play basketball or hockey with them in the evening. When the officers go for a run, they need to show that they can do all that they ask the troops to do and do it better. That's the only way you can earn the respect of your team members. Every officer has to know everything about the troops they work with. That is why a soldier will lay down his life at the command of the officer. He knows that his boss will make sure his family is looked after long after he is gone.'

Balwanpur was a typical small town. There was no anonymity possible, for anybody. I realized that when I went to the barber's for a haircut. The solitary barber's chair held a customer who was getting a shave. As soon as I walked in, the barber unceremoniously stopped and told the man to wait while he finished my haircut. The more I protested that it wasn't necessary and I could wait, the more the man whom I had displaced seemed to squirm. He told me that he was Nirmal, a shift electrician, and it was okay for him to wait. My time was more precious, he said. Eventually I realized that the best thing to do was to get on with my haircut and stop holding up other customers – at least until someone senior came along to displace me.

Nirmal waited with shaving foam clinging to one side of his face while the barber gave me a leisurely haircut and head massage. As I was leaving, he told me that most officers had him go over to their house for a haircut and that I should do the same in future. Maybe this was what Captain Sobti meant when he exhorted me to become a big fish. If the incident at the barber's shop was anything to go by, I was probably well on my way to becoming one.

But first, I had to get the workers to start feeling comfortable with me. In a strange way, I had to learn to get comfortable with them as well. No real communication could take place otherwise. I began to join the workers in their canteen and eat lunch with them. Initially there would be silence as soon as I joined a table. I would attempt to start a conversation, but no one seemed keen to talk. Instead, they would start to grill me. They wanted to know all about my life and school and college, and about Baba, Ma and Asmita. What did I miss, now that I was in Balwanpur? I noticed that they all took a certain sense of pride in being part of the township. They were surprised that I missed Delhi.

'Balwanpur has everything that you would find in Delhi. We have our own cinema hall. The parks are well maintained. We are like one big family. What makes you think that Delhi is better? The managers' club here must be better than any you would find in Delhi. So what do you miss?'

I had no way of explaining to them why I missed the city lights. The buzz that came from walking down Janpath and having coffee on a lazy afternoon. Or browsing in the second-hand bookstores. The lanes of Chandni Chowk. The Railway Colony. And, I missed Ayesha.

'I miss having jalebis at Chandni Chowk,' I said one day.

'Come over to my house and my wife will make jalebis for you,' said Sohanlal Negi, who had come to Balwanpur Industries twenty years ago with his father and had stayed on after he found a job on the shopfloor as an operative. In course of time, due to his ability to negotiate difficult situations, Sohanlal became the logical choice to take over the leadership of the Workers' Union of Balwanpur. He was now also the president of the Balwanpur Employees' Union. The workers seemed to worship him. He had never let them down and they knew he could reach Captain Sobti at a moment's notice.

Sohanlal Negi explained that the first sign of prosperity among the workers was having at least two heads of cattle at home. It was the norm to serve a guest hot milk or cool lassi. Serving tea meant that financial success had eluded the host. So, whenever I was invited to a worker's home, I was to always start the conversation with enquiries regarding the cattle owned by the host. He would then ask me for a choice of lassi or milk. That was the tradition.

Negi's invitation to me was a sign that I had been accepted by the employees of Balwanpur. That opened the floodgates. I was hardly ever home in the evenings. Every night I was at a worker's home for dinner. On Sundays I would play golf with Captain Sobti. I was also a regular invitee at any wedding or celebration that took place.

Living in the township was like taking a crash course in human resources. Captain Sobti had told me that the unspoken rule of the Officers' Complex was that the hierarchy in the office applied equally to all social interaction. I thanked God that there was no Mrs Sobti for me – or my wife, should I marry sometime soon – to suck up to. The very thought made me sick.

One day, when I was trying to get some paperwork out of the way, I got a call from Balwan Singh's office. I was to immediately meet 'Singh Madam'. I was told in hushed tones that Singh Madam was Mrs Mohini Singh, his wife. I rushed as commanded, quite dreading what lay ahead. But she turned out to be rather pleasant to talk to.

'Hello, beta. I have heard so much about you from Singh saab. I need your help to saalv a praablem.'

The problem was an interesting one. The company provided free cable television to the town's residents. In the morning, from six to seven, they aired religious sermons given by the spiritual guru to the Singh family – Swami Krishna Anand Guru. In the afternoon, they would show tapes of India's first TV soap, *Hum Log*. Then, starting 4 p.m., three Hindi films would be telecast. There were rumblings from the Workers' Housing Complex that these films were causing havoc. Several of the workers' children had failed their school exams. Yet, cable TV was the only source of joy in the entertainment starved town of Balwanpur. And there was no way of selectively offering it to some and not to the others. It was an either or problem, as they used to say at MIJ. Either they all got it or no one would.

I tried talking to several of the concerned groups, but they were all equally rigid and aggressive in their demand. I fretted about it for a while, then asked Captain Sobti for help.

He leaned back in his chair and said, 'That is easy. Send a register to every house and ask them to write down the names of their children and then mention if they have passed or failed in the exam. Depending on the number of children who have failed, we can take a decision on whether to continue or discontinue the cable service.' He smiled mysteriously.

We sent someone from my office to each of the five thousand workers' homes to identify the children who had flunked. Three days later, the man returned with a blank register. According to it, none of the kids had flunked. And so the problem of TV or no TV was resolved. I remembered again, Haathi's line: 'Problems cannot be solved. They can be absolved, resolved or dissolved.'

On Sundays I used to call up Baba-Ma and talk to them about my life here. Ayesha was enjoying herself too. She told me how they had celebrated Diwali by having a sort of MIJ reunion in Delhi. Joy, Gur, Neats, Arunesh and Gopher were all there. Funny was on a trip abroad. He was spending a week in Nepal.

'Gur and Neetika are getting married next month. You must come over. It's been almost a year since you came to Delhi. We'll go to this great disco called the Cellar.'

'Ayesha, why don't you come over here for a chhutti? You'll love it. The place is beautiful and the people are wonderful.'

'Abbey, I am going to Manali with some colleagues. Apparently, cannabis grows wild in that area.'

'Is that boss of yours going too?'

I had to speak louder than usual because of the awful phone connection. But I thought I heard Ayesha say yes to that last question.

On the way home, I met Mrs Dayal who was going for a walk with Funtoosh. There had been an interesting reconciliation over the last few months. Mrs Dayal took charge of my life. She sent me dinner every Sunday. In return, Funtoosh used my garden to express his opinion about life and people in general. In fact, Mrs Dayal once mentioned that had she met me a year ago, she would have got her daughter married to me. That was the only time I heard her referring to her daughter who was married to some hot-shot corporate executive.

One day, she showed me a photograph of her daughter and Mr Dayal (I presumed), taken at some hill station.

'That was taken when my daughter Muniya turned five. She wanted to go to Switzerland to see the snow. We

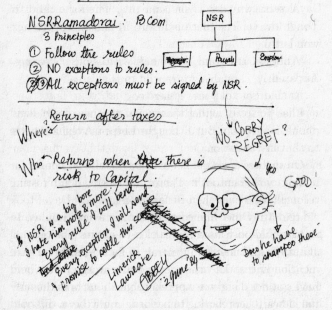

*Introduction to Finance*

<u>NSR Ramadorai</u> : BCom

3 Principles

① Follow the rules

② NO exceptions to rules.

②③ All exceptions must be signed by NSR.

NSR

Regan. | Payали | Employ

Where's <u>Return after taxes</u>

Who → Returns when <del>the</del> there is risk to Capital.

NO SORRY REGRET?

Yes

GOOD.

* NSR is a big bore
I hate him more & more
Every rule I will send
Every exception I will send
I promise to settle this score

Limerick Laureate

ABEY "2 June '84"

Does he have to shampoo these

could not afford a foreign trip. So we went to Kausani – the Switzerland of India. That is Mount Trishul in the background,' she said as she dusted the solitary photo in her drawing room and put it back lovingly.

'So where is Muniya now?'

'I'll tell you about it some day. But not now.' Mrs Dayal seemed upset as she said this. Then she tried to change the topic rather obviously by asking how things were between Rajani and me.

'What about Rajani? I met her here the other evening, that's all.'

'Ramadorai told me yesterday that your horoscope matches perfectly with Rajani's and that she really likes you. He is so fussy about all this horoscope matching. That's why, even though Rajani really liked that young man Sankaran, they could not get married because his horoscope did not match hers. At least now Ramadorai doesn't seem so fussed about having a Bengali son-in-law.'

I told Mrs Dayal immediately and in no uncertain terms that I would only marry a girl of my parents' choice, and that anyway, I had no intention of getting married just yet. The line about my parents really worked with her, but I could tell she was apprehensive about breaking the bad news to her boss. Ramadorai could be a difficult colleague to deal with, she warned me. She had seen him making life difficult for anybody he disliked. I told her I was not going to let that decide my choice of spouse and quickly tried to divert her attention with some office gossip.

'So tell me about Balwan Singh's family. What does he do with the truckloads of money he makes?'

'He runs the whole township. Every year he starts work on a new school or a dispensary. Last year he built a huge park with lovely fountains. The only thing that is missing is a good college. If I hadn't had to send Muniya to college in Delhi, things would have been perfect. Have you met Balwan Singhji's daughter? She's so pretty. I wish you would marry her.'

'Mrs Dayal, you really should stop matchmaking. I am already engaged to someone,' I lied just to get away from this strange problem. 'There is a girl called Keya who I knew when I was doing my MBA. I am supposed to marry her.'

'So where is my soon-to-be bahu?'

'She is in Delhi. I must go now. It's getting late.' I had to escape this inquisition.

The truth of the matter was that I had written to Keya, at her address in Jamshedpur, asking her when she would come to Delhi. The last time I saw her, running alongside the train as it pulled out of Jampot, she had said that she would be coming in August. Maybe she had changed her mind. All I knew was that even the memory of Keya opened up wounds deep within me, so I had pushed her out of mind's reach.

I could tell from Ramadorai's behaviour exactly when Mrs Dayal conveyed my decision to him. He sent me a typewritten memo saying that the circular he had sent me regarding the suitcase and the crockery set applied only to employees who had joined before 31 December 1983. I realized then that he would keep finding legally valid irritants to prove to me that I had made a blunder by not marrying his beloved daughter.

The next day, I called up Ayesha and told her that I was going to be in Delhi on a 'business trip' and would love to catch up with her.

I was scheduled to go to Delhi a week later with Captain Sobti for a meeting with some government officials. More than anything else, I was excited about being able to stay in a five-star hotel even though I could have easily stayed at home with my parents.

I called home and announced that I was in Delhi and staying at the Taj. Asmita wanted to know if I would treat them to dinner at the hotel.

'Of course! You will be my guests. Please make sure that Baba and Ma are dressed for the occasion. And you could wear that blue salwar kameez you got for your birthday. You may bump into my boss, Captain Sobti. Please, Ass, tell Baba-Ma not to call me Chotka in front of my colleagues.' I had to give all my instructions to my parents through my sister.

When Baba, Ma and Asmita arrived that evening, I received them in the lobby. Everyone looked dressed to go for a wedding reception. We walked to the restaurant and sat down in silence. Captain Sobti walked in then and I stood up to introduce him.

'Baba, Ma, and this is my kid sister Asmita. This is Captain Sobti, our Personnel Manager.' My parents did a namaskar while Asmita shook hands.

Baba proceeded to make the first faux pas. 'I hope Chotka is working hard. Please make sure you show no leniency towards him. This is the time to build the foundations of his career. Hard work must be the only thing you expect from him.'

'Abbey is our brightest young manager,' said Captain Sobti with a smile. 'He has set an example for others with his hard work and ability to blend with the team. This meeting with the ministry we've come for is being entirely handled by him. You must be very proud parents.' He looked at his watch. 'I must go now, but please come and visit us in Balwanpur.' He pulled me aside just before leaving and whispered, 'Dinner is on me. Please send me the bill and spare no expenses.'

My mother had tears in her eyes. Tears of joy, as Ass was quick to explain to me.

Baba was also speechless for a while and then said, 'This place is very expensive. Let's just have a cup of tea and go. There is food at home. Don't waste your money here. You must save for a rainy day.'

'Chotka can afford to treat us here. That's why he has invited us,' Ma said quietly. 'But tonight's dinner is a treat from us, Baba and me.'

'But it's paid for by your company, isn't that what you told me?' Asmita was surprised at this sudden turn of events.

'Okay, then please eat frugally. The company must not think that Chotka has acted irresponsibly just because they are paying for the meal.' Baba had to have the last word.

Dinner was a grand affair. Two hours after we had sat down, coffee was brought to the table, and just then Ayesha sauntered in with a middle-aged man. She was the first to notice me.

'Abbey! You dog! You came to town and didn't even call.'

'Ayesha, meet my parents. And this is Asmita, my kid sister. Baba-Ma, Ayesha is my classmate from MIJ.' Dad looked fairly disapprovingly at Ayesha's outfit.

'Hello!' said Ayesha. 'This is Kevin, my landlord. He is flying back to New York tonight. I came to drop him off at the hotel, where he's meeting his colleagues.'

Kevin stepped up and said, 'Ayesha, why don't you catch up with your friends and I will get a drink with my gang. Nice meeting you. Bye.'

'Let's order some ice cream for Ayesha. Chotka keeps talking about you,' Ma said in a loving tone.

For the next half hour Ayesha behaved in a manner that really surprised me. She was all coy and charming. She complimented Asmita on her dress and said that blue was her favourite colour too. She talked to Baba about her uncle in Badhwar Park who worked for the Western Railway and with whom she had stayed when she did her summer training. She asked Ma if she could come over and learn how to make ilish maachh. After a while, even

Baba thawed, but I continued to be on tenterhooks, ready to jump in at a moment's notice.

We were interrupted by the waiter bringing us a large, beautifully decorated chocolate cake. The accompanying card said, 'With compliments from K.'

'That is so nice of Mr Kevin,' said Baba.

'It must be imported chocolate,' said Asmita.

'I must go home now. Delhi is not a safe city for a girl alone, Uncle.' Ayesha hugged Asmita and Ma and did a polite namaskar to Baba.

'You must come home and I will teach you all the recipes that you want to learn,' said Ma.

After Ayesha left, I began to breathe normally again. I asked for the bill and then escorted Baba, Ma and Asmita to a cab.

Asmita winked at me and whispered, 'Ayesha is really gorgeous. Good choice.' I reached out to yank her pigtail but she was already in the cab.

I walked into my room to find a huge bouquet of pink gladioli tied with a red ribbon. Beside it sat a box of Godiva chocolates and a small envelope from which I pulled out a white card with a message that said, 'Wishing you and Ayesha the very best – K.'

# Six

I met Captain Sobti for breakfast the next morning. I knew about his obsession with punctuality, so I got there at 8:29 a.m. sharp. I joined him at the table and handed over the bill for last night's dinner.

'Good morning, Abbey. Sit down, you're out of breath. Running late, eh? You're clearly not a very organized person. But glad you could have a nice evening with your parents. They obviously adore you.'

'Thanks for saying all those nice things about me.'

'Praising an employee in front of his parents is the second biggest recognition opportunity. Praising him in front of his wife and kids is the first. It makes an employee walk tall in the office. Which reminds me, have you signed the bill for the annual day of Balwanpur High School?'

'Yes, I did. But tell me, Captain, why isn't there a single college in Balwanpur? I can't say that Balwan Singh is not committed to the cause of education: we have eleven middle and high schools.'

Captain Sobti sipped his orange juice and lit a cigar. He thought for a moment before answering my question.

'Elementary, dear Watson. The schools ensure a steady supply of workforce for Balwanpur Industries. Yet, the kids are not educated enough to find options outside. Most of the managers in Balwanpur studied in these schools and then started working here. They will never find a better job anywhere else. So nobody ever leaves Balwanpur to work for someone else. We actively encourage the employees' children to work for us too. The whole family is then working for the company and everyone's fortunes are intertwined. That is one important reason why we have never had a strike.'

'The trade union we have is said to be a puppet union. Is that true, Captain?'

'Negi is as independent as anybody else. But over the years the workers have realized that even if they form a union, it is the management that finally signs the cheque. So they are better off trusting us. The truth is, it is good for their egoes to have a union. They feel like they are big boys. By the way, who was that pretty lady at your table last evening?'

'You mean Asmita?'

'No, the one who joined you later. I believe her name is Ayesha.'

'How do you know her name? I thought you had left by then.' Captain Sobti always surprised me with his ability to read my mind.

'You've written everybody's name on this bill. The only one I don't recognize is Ayesha. Am I right in thinking there's some good news round the corner?'

'I don't know... actually... it's nothing... I have never... Ayesha is just...' I tried several different ways to begin the sentence but failed.

'We have to find excuses to send you to Delhi more often, now that you will need to meet Ayesha,' said Sobti with a twinkle in his eye.

I met Ayesha the next day. Her apartment seemed even more posh in comparison to my spartan dwellings in Balwanpur. She had just emerged from the shower. I inhaled her freshly shampooed hair and we kissed.

I told her what Captain Sobti had said.

'So there must be some truth to it. But hey, if you want to propose to me, Abbey, you have to go down on your knees and do it right. Where's the ring you are going to give me? Or, maybe, just maybe, I should be the one going down on my knees.'

'Ayesha... ouch... you mean you will marry me? You actually want to... oh man... mmmm... Should I? Oh God!' The rest of the conversation was what you might call spiritual, punctuated with moans and plenty of breathless silence.

I told Ma about wanting to marry Ayesha. I had to borrow money from her for a wedding ring if I planned to propose that evening. Ma opened her almirah and took out a small ring, at the centre of which was a tiny star-shaped diamond.

'We have a little tradition. In our family, the mother-in-law hands over a ring to the eldest child. This belonged to my grandmother. I want to pass it on to Ayesha.' Ma handed me the ring in a small velvet box.

'So if I were older than you, this would have come to me?' Asmita enquired.

'I'll buy one for you when you get married,' I assured her.

Baba remained sceptical about my ability to manage a family. 'Chotka, I am not sure you are ready to move on to grahastha ashram just yet. You've barely learned to take charge of yourself. You still need someone to wake you up in the morning. How you manage to get to work on time, I don't know. And now you want to get married to this Punjabi girl! Punjabi girls are so oversmart. Will she continue working after marriage or will she live with you in Balwanpur?'

'Baba, to be honest, I haven't asked her if she will continue to work after marriage. As a matter of fact, I have not even proposed to her. Should I just call it off?' I asked. I was beginning to have doubts myself.

Ma stepped in. 'Of course not. Ayesha is an MBA. They will make a lovely couple. Whether she works after marriage or not is for them to decide. You don't have to interfere,' she scolded Baba. Asmita sniggered in the background.

And so, I did propose to Ayesha and she accepted. I had never seen her so happy. We called up our erstwhile batchmates and had a wild party, MIJ style. It was hosted by Pappu. We put on the old albums that were favourites from our days in the hostel. Pappu kept playing the

Queen number 'Another one bites the dust' till I begged for mercy.

By now, Pappu was sloshed as a chimpanzee. He took me aside and said philosophically, 'I know you are missing Keya. You have made a choice and moved on. Now forget Keya.'

'My God, how did you read my mind? I was just thinking of Keya. I wonder where she is. Anyway, it's too late now. She did tell me that she was coming to Delhi, but she didn't contact me even once. Do you know, I wrote to her at her address in Jampot, but I don't think the letter reached her. Or maybe it did, and she chose not to respond. Shit! Now here I am, marrying Ayesha. Isn't that great? I always thought she would marry some crazy rich tycoon. But she is marrying this middle-class Bong. Your glass is empty, bastard. Make another strong one for me.'

Pappu filled two glasses and came back to cleverly change the topic. 'Abbey, just listen to apna Mercury. The bugger is so bloody talented. Hear the warning, bastard.'

There are plenty of ways you can hurt a man
And bring him to the ground
You can beat him
You can cheat him
You can treat him bad and leave him
When he's down
But I'm ready, yes I'm ready for you.

There was plenty of OM2 served up in a drum and we all drank ourselves silly. The wedding was fixed for 14 February.

The Marriage Registrar was available only at 9 a.m. in the morning. When he did arrive, he was in a hurry. Evidently, Valentine's Day was a popular choice for a wedding day, so he had limited time. He fished out a set of forms and gave them to Ayesha to fill. The bunch of relatives who had landed up at my place gathered around to witness the event. Gulshan, the photographer from Railway Colony, had organized a video camera to film it all in loving detail. Ayesha filled up her form pretty fast until she came to the place where it wanted to know 'Status of the bride at the time of marriage'. She looked at me and asked silently what the answer should be. I shrugged ignorance. All my relatives were hovering around, holding their breath. She shrugged back and wrote 'Virgin'. When it came to my turn to answer the same question, I asked the Registrar what the options were. He looked at me, made a face and said, 'Just write that you are unmarried.'

Ayesha's parents had booked the Banquet Hall at the Taj and employed a Wedding Event Coordinator who had organized everything like clockwork. They had hired a Mercedes Benz to cart me from my house to the hotel. Each time I looked out and caught a glimpse of the garishly decorated car, I cringed inwardly. My parents had invited all our relatives from Calcutta, so the house was full of guests. Asmita joined me in the Merc as we drove to the venue. Sharmila Tagore and Pataudi were the star attractions at the wedding. Apparently, Pataudi and Ayesha's dad had met on a flight to Germany some years ago and had become good friends. Our side of the family had no such celebrities to boast of. So we showed off our relatives in full strength.

The entire gang of MIJ had been invited. And the grand surprise was Rascal Rusty, who happened to be in India en route to the US. He had flown down from Dubai with a bottle of Chivas Regal gift-wrapped for us. He looked prosperous and his visiting card told us that he was now a vice president.

The wedding was something to remember, said everyone. Baba, Ma and all our relatives stuck together. I don't know if they were having a good time, but Ayesha's parents were certainly drinking and dancing with all their invitees. Get a few north Indians together in a celebratory mood and inevitably they will switch to the lowest common denominator, aka bhangra. Okay, I like doing the bhangra too, but how long can you keep your hands up in the air as though you're trying to change a light bulb?

Ayesha wore a low-cut blouse with strings at the back that pretty much drew the attention of everyone. She was weighed down with gold and diamond jewellery and her mauve-coloured lehenga sparkled with gold threadwork. As we stood together, greeting the guests, she whispered to me, 'So how do I look?'

'Like a Christmas tree. Only Santa is missing,' I whispered back. I thought that was clever.

'Your beer belly certainly makes you look like Santa!' Ayesha's retort was unexpectedly sharp.

Lesson learnt. Ayesha was no longer a classmate or a girlfriend. She was the wife.

My aunt pulled me aside then and said that (a) as per our family's tradition it was blasphemy to have the bride do a bhangra with the guests, and (b) could I please ask Ayesha not to drink in the presence of my parents.

The following day, Baba and Ma hosted a reception at the club in the Railway Colony at Sardar Patel Marg, as was the tradition in our neighbourhood. Ayesha went through the whole ceremony without any fuss, and I was grateful for that. Ramaswamy and his sons put up a dosa counter, which was a rocking hit. All my old pals from the colony were there. The club had been done up with tiny lamps and it felt like Diwali. The MIJ gang was there in full strength, again. Arunesh had brought his guitar and performed to a large and admiring audience. The hottest chick in our colony, Divya Samtani and her dad, who was also the secretary of the club, stood up close, requesting Kishore Kumar numbers, while the MIJ boys basked in reflected glory. Only my oldest friends, Kapil and Priya, were missing. Kapil was in Kanpur representing a client; he worked for an accountancy firm now. And Priya did not land up. After our last meeting, an awkwardness had crept into our relationship: we were cordial, but strangely formal with each other.

Ayesha's parents and their relatives were visibly disappointed that there was no alcohol at the reception.

After hanging round aimlessly for a while, they told us they had to leave early since they had to take an early morning flight. I saw Ayesha talking to each of them, trying to persuade them to stay back for dinner.

'My relatives behave like bloody addicts. I know they are all going to hit some bar to drink themselves silly. Sometimes they can be really insensitive. What do we tell your parents, Abbey? Oh damn, I'd better do it.'

As Ayesha explained the situation to my parents, my relatives played Chinese whispers with each other. Baba couldn't conceal how upset he was. The only one who remained composed was Ma.

'They have a flight to catch tomorrow morning. It is not a good idea to eat all this Bengali food. It is very heavy. They have had the snacks and dosas. Ayesha, have you had dinner? You look tired. Why don't you and Chotka have dinner? Let me go and see if the guests have had the doi-mishti.' My mother, the star. No matter how many guests there were, she always seemed to be in control.

I don't think anybody can enjoy their own wedding. I certainly didn't. There were too many things to be done, too many egos to be managed, too many loose ends to be tied. It was past midnight when Ayesha and I reached home.

'I can't believe we are married. Hello, husband! Do you always wear a silk kurta pajama at night, or is this just to impress me?' said Ayesha as she slid into bed and hugged me from behind.

'Hey, this is our big night. Don't I need to dress up to look my best?'

According to Bengali tradition, tonight was our 'first night'. The bed had been decorated with flowers and there was a bouquet of red roses from Kevin that said, 'Sure you will be happy ToGetHer – K'.

Only, we were too tired to do anything but hold hands and fall asleep.

# SEVEN

We went to Conoor for our honeymoon. This erstwhile summer resort of the British is a quaint little town tucked away among the tea gardens in the Nilgiri Hills. The Garden Retreat was a place designed for the lazy. Ayesha and I spent most days lying in the hammocks in the garden, getting up only for important chores like fetching more beer. There was a lovely cherry tree in the middle of the garden that actually had red cherries hanging from the low branches.

On the second day, it started to rain early in the morning. Ayesha and I lay in bed under the sheets, listening to the raindrops. She made a pillow out of my left hand and moved in closer. I could smell her perfume. I ran my fingers through her hair as she put her chin on my chest and looked at me.

'I can hear your heartbeat, Abbey.'

I had never seen her eyes so close. They looked a warm shade of chocolate. I ran my fingers along the curve of her face and her body arched in pleasure. In the background, Kishore Kumar's voice rose clear: 'Pal pal dil ke paas, tum rehti ho…'

In the afternoon, Ayesha and I pulled up two rocking chairs and sat near the large French windows, watching the raindrops fall on the cobbled path and run away in snaking rivulets. We drank steaming Malabar coffee in oversized mugs and chatted. Later, downstairs, in the dining room, we met a group of French tourists who were all talking excitedly about some place called Erin Villa.

So, armed with the address, Ayesha and I visited Erin Villa, a hundred year-old house located right in the middle of Singara Estate. It was a quaint little villa with cupids in the garden and marble statues of 'topless women', as they might say at MIJ. There were gardens within gardens, separated by little gates. Ayesha knew the names of most of the flowers. I showed off my limited knowledge of the three flowers that I could identify as dahlia, hibiscus and bougainvillea.

A week passed quickly and soon it was time to get back to reality. I had to return to work. Ayesha still had two weeks of vacation ahead of her.

We got a royal welcome when we reached the apartment at Balwanpur. Captain Sobti had sanctioned an extra bed and a telephone. Balwan Singh had gifted us a small colour television. I had invited all my colleagues in the department and all the other departmental heads for a party in the evening. Two of the directors came. Balwan Singh drove up in his black

BMW and the photographer captured the moment on celluloid.

In the days that followed, my colleagues went out of their way to make Ayesha feel welcome. She and I were invited out for dinner every evening. What touched me the most was a dinner invitation from Sohanlal Negi and his wife. They laid out a rather elaborate home-cooked dinner that ended with piping hot jalebis. A small crowd of curious onlookers peeked in through the window to catch a glimpse of Ayesha who was dressed in a salwar kameez (with a dupatta) and some delicate silver jewellery. When we were about to leave, Sohanlal and his wife presented us with a sewing machine. It was a gift from the workers of Balwanpur Industries.

The next day, I decided to show Ayesha the major tourist attractions of the township.

'There is the mansion that Balwan Singh lives in, and next to that you have the Directors' Housing Complex where the big four live.'

'Okay, so your boss lives in the Senior Managers' Housing Complex, the workers have their own complex. What is this housing complex called where we live?'

'The Inferiority Complex?' I suggested

Ayesha and I would spend the evenings going for long, lazy walks until the sun made way for the moon. There was so much we had to say to each other, so much to understand. I discovered that she had taken lessons in oil painting for three years, and that she had a fascination for phobias.

'You don't know a person until you know what their phobias are,' she said one evening. 'People have the most unusual phobias. I have thanatophobia – the fear of dying. Comes from the Greek word, thanatos, meaning death instinct. Some phobias sound the same but are very different. For example, agoraphobia is the fear of unfamiliar spaces but agraphobia is the fear of sexual abuse. What are you afraid of, Abbey?'

'I am afraid of not having enough sex. What's that called? Inadequatesexophobia?'

Ayesha punched me on the arm and said, 'Captain Sobti has ophidiophobia – the fear of snakes. Do you know, he is so paranoid about snakes that he can't even bear to play snakes and ladders? It was so fascinating to see such a tough-looking man go all queasy at the mention of how I had almost died of snakebite as a child. In fact, and even you may not know this, Abbey, he has hired two hundred members of the Irula tribe of Tamil Nadu and employed them as workmen in the factory. He told me the word "Irula" comes from "Irul", the Tamil word for darkness. Since the Irulas lived in the forest, that term stuck. Many Irulas have traditionally earned their living as snake catchers. Their brief is to make sure that Balwanpur is snake free.'

Ayesha was like a walking dictionary of phobias. She believed that I had sesquipedalophobia – the fear of long words.

Every morning, I would wake up to the smell of freshly brewed coffee and put on a cassette of Nikhil Banerjee playing

Raga Ahir Bhairav on the sitar. Over the soft notes, all you could hear was the chirping of birds. Not so far away, we would hear the crowing of the rooster and the sound of cow bells as the cattle were readied for the day ahead.

There were some surprises too. Like one evening, I came back home to hear loud music playing, apparently from my apartment. The living room had been turned into a discotheque. The furniture had been moved and there were four young men in the room, whom I recognized as engineering trainees. I also recognized Rajani, who waved to me. Ayesha did the same. I was a bit nonplussed and wondered if I should go into the bedroom and let the party fizzle out. Rajani beckoned me to dance with her. I walked up reluctantly. I did not like being forced to do anything – not even to party.

'I had to lie to my dad and say that I was visiting Dayal Aunty. Meet my friends, Chithra alias Chitty, and that's Padmini Bisht, Paddy for short, and that's Shashikala, we call her Shash. Remember the gang from Stella Maris I told you about? They were visiting Balwanpur and we bumped into Ayesha at the club. She told us to come over. Honestly, Ayesha is such a welcome addition to the township.'

'I am sorry if I hurt you in any way, Rajani. Mr Ramadorai moved in with horoscopes and what not. I just wasn't prepared for that. I hope you understand.'

'I understand. But dad doesn't. He is really sore with you. I guess he is worried about me. You see, I lost my mother when I was in class eight. Since then, dad has been hyper-protective. Hey, I think Paddy likes you. Maybe you should dance with her. Remember we need to be back home by 9 p.m.'

Later that night, when Ayesha and I were lying in bed, I asked her why she had not warned me about the party earlier in the evening.

She looked at me and said sarcastically, 'Sorry, O Lord and Master. I will put in a written application next time. It is your house, after all.'

The conversation could have turned ugly. I told her that she should not have invited the trainees. If Ramadorai got to know that his daughter had been here, he would go crazy. At the end of my impassioned five-minute lecture, I realized I didn't have an audience: Ayesha was fast asleep. Too much booze, I guess.

Ma would call up sometimes to enquire how Ayesha was managing. Ayesha would take meticulous notes on recipes. Eventually she managed to make rice and daal, much to my surprise. Mrs Dayal continued with her self-appointed role of caterer; for those fourteen days that Ayesha was there, she doubled the quantity.

On the day that she was to return to Delhi, Ayesha pulled on her tight jeans and mauve T-Shirt that said 'It is your lucky day today'. An Ambassador had been hired to drive her back. She packed her stuff into the snazzy suitcases her dad had brought for her from the US. When she finished packing, we went to our bedroom and made love before she took the cab back to her apartment in Connaught Place.

I lay down on my back and stared at the ceiling fan. I missed Ayesha already. I missed my wife. I missed chatting with her. She had the ability to bring life into any conversation and had everyone eating out of her hands as soon as she started talking. It was probably her sense of humour that allowed her to charm even her sharpest critics. I poured myself a large swig of OM2 and wondered if she regretted marrying me. In my eyes, Ayesha would always remain the saucy classmate who was every male's fantasy at MIJ. There was a part of me that disbelieved the fact that she had actually married me. I wondered if she would ever stop being a trophy that I could show off. Even in the two weeks that she was around, she had become the talk of the town. The men would give her admiring looks and the women would look at her and mentally compare themselves with her (and usually fall short). And it felt so good when she linked hands with me as we walked or talked to people. Did she feel the same?

The phone rang, waking me up with a start.

'Hi, sweetheart. I am missing you like mad,' I slurred.

'Hello Chotka, has Ayesha reached Delhi? We are getting worried. I had told her to call and let me know. What's the address of her flat in Connaught Place? I have made some food for her. Ishsh... I hope she is not hungry.'

'Ma, sorry. I thought you were Ayesha. She will be okay, don't worry. She called some time back to tell me she had reached and that she has had dinner.' I was lying, of course.

'Chotka, she is my daughter-in-law. I must look after my little bouma.' It was the first time I had heard Ma refer to Ayesha as her bouma – Bengali for daughter-in-law. 'Ayesha is hardly half an hour away from our house. You must ask her to stay with us if she feels comfortable. Of course, it will add to her commute.' Ma always provided a face-saving way out. She passed the phone to Baba.

'Hello! Did you take the day off? You could have gone back to the office after bouma left. Do not fritter away your earned leave. Save it and then encash it at year-end,' Baba suggested.

I replied in monosyllables to avoid slurring. I wondered what Baba's reaction would be if he knew I was semi-drunk. Asmita tried to cheer me up by telling me a joke. I could sense their concern for me. They knew I was lonely and missing Ayesha. All at once, I was filled with gratitude that I belonged to such a close-knit family.

Twenty-four hours after Ayesha left, I still hadn't heard from her. When I called her office, she answered on the second ring.

'Ayesha, I was worried sick. Why the fuck didn't you call me after you reached Delhi? Ma-Baba were worried too, yaar. Give them a call and let them know you are okay.'

'Maybe I should pay for an ad on Doordarshan to tell the world that Ayesha has arrived safely. Stop sounding like my grandma, Abbey. You Bongs are a really paranoid race. What did you think I was up to? Having sex with someone else?'

'I don't know about voluntary sex, but there's plenty of involuntary sex you could get dragged into, especially in Delhi. Anyway, forget it. Let's talk of something pleasant.'

'I need to go for a meeting. I'll call you later.'

'Listen, don't forget to call Baba-Ma sometime today,' I said. But she had disconnected the phone.

I spoke to Asmita that evening to check if Ayesha had called them.

'She must have been busy. Don't worry, I told Ma that Ayesha had spoken to me from the office and apologized for not calling the previous evening. I think I'll go over to her apartment one day and surprise her. Do you know, Bhai, Divya Samtani – you know, that snooty girl in our colony – has also got into MIJ. You should have seen her at the club last evening. She's such a disgusting show-off. Her dad treated everyone to dosas and coffee.'

From Ass's daily updates, it appeared that life in the Railway Colony was moving at the same uncomplicated pace as it always had.

Here at Balwanpur, in my apartment, I had to get used to living alone. Even the house seemed to smell different. When the dhobi returned a set of freshly ironed clothes the day after Ayesha left, I looked at them and missed her even more. I picked up a bottle of perfume that she had left in front of the large mirror in our bedroom and sprayed some on to a swab of cotton. The fragrance brought her back to me for a moment.

The only way I could keep my mind off Ayesha's

absence was by focussing on my work. Captain Sobti was pleased with my progress. On the first of June, exactly a year after I had joined the company, I got my first promotion at work. I became Assistant Manager, Personnel. I called Ayesha and told her about it.

'That's wonderful, Abbey. I'll call my parents right away, and yours too. They'll be so happy. Come on over this weekend, darling. We must celebrate.'

Captain Sobti sent me to Delhi for some meetings, armed with a cake for Ayesha. She met me at the Railway Colony house, suitcase in hand. Baba and Ma were thrilled to see us. The next morning, Ayesha and I left for work together and came back in time for dinner. Ma made sure the dining table was loaded with Ayesha's favourite dishes. Asmita and Ayesha watched *Chitrahaar* on TV, giggling as they watched the Bollywood song-and-dance numbers. In the days that followed, the routine held. Ayesha would chat with Baba, Ma and Ass for hours and would have them rolling with laughter as she narrated stories from her school days.

I am afraid I can't say the same for the way I handled Ayesha's family. I know one is supposed to start liking, if not loving one's in-laws, or at least make an honest attempt at it, but Ayesha's parents were weird people. Whenever I met them, all their conversation was with Ayesha. Her dad would offer me a drink, after which the whole family would continue talking and laughing among themselves as if I did not exist.

Like that one Sunday when Ayesha's parents flew down

from Jamshedpur to Delhi for the weekend. They did not stay with us despite repeated requests from my parents. They did come over with gifts for everyone and invited us all to join them for dinner at the Taj. My mother insisted that we eat at home and prepared a splendid meal that would have put the hotel's buffet to shame. But the evening was a disaster. The contrast was too stark. Ayesha's father arrived wearing a business suit that looked expensive. Her mother wore a pair of slacks and a garish yellow top with geometric patterns on it. Her handbag was made of snake or alligator skin. Each time she touched her coiffured hair, her diamond earrings flashed. She evaluated the entire house with one glance before putting on an artificial smile.

Baba, dressed in a freshly starched kurta pajama, escorted them to the drawing room. Ma had made sure that every brass figure on display was gleaming. Asmita had prominently displayed a replica of the Statue of Liberty that my cousin Khokon had brought back for us from his first trip to New York.

'What can we offer you?' Baba asked.

Ayesha's father laughed politely and said, 'My wife only likes Scotch, but I will happily drink anything from your bar – even if it is Indian whisky. Of course, we should let our son-in-law decide these things. The kids know more about whisky than we do.'

That last remark caught me completely off-guard. I don't know about Ma, but Baba certainly did not know anything about my preferences. My family only bred teetotallers and any mention of alcohol was taboo. It was looked down upon as something that villains in Hindi films drank before they molested the heroine. There was no question of serving alcohol in our household. At home, when someone was offered a choice of drink, it was either coffee or tea.

'Asmita has baked a cake for you. Let's have some tea and cake first,' Ma suggested, much to the relief of Baba, as she disappeared into the kitchen with Asmita.

'Dad, you need to try the cake and tea combo. Asmita is famous for her cakes,' Ayesha chipped in.

'You people are very British in your behaviour, I can see. Tea and cake in the evening,' said Ayesha's father.

'Not at all,' said Baba emphatically, 'my father and grandfather were freedom fighters. My father-in-law's brother was Naresh Roy, who masterminded the Chittagong Armoury Raid along with Surya Sen. We are not at all British in any way, and are proud to be Indian.'

Seriously, there was no need to do that last bit. I tried to step into the conversation but it was impossible. Asmita brought in cake and tea. We all got busy trying to eat. Except Ayesha's mother, who would not eat the cake despite a million exhortations from everyone.

'I have a bit of gambler's blood in me,' Ayesha's dad said casually to Baba. 'I've bought a beachfront property in Kerala and a cottage near Simla. But my wife tells me that until you have a summer home in Europe, life is not complete. That's the task she has put me on to! How about you? Are you interested in buying stocks and shares or do you prefer to invest in real estate?'

'You know how meagre government salaries are. We have a small flat in Calcutta. Buying that meant taking a massive loan from my Provident Fund. Then, when Chotka went to MIJ, I had to take a loan for that as well. Where is the money to buy property? I have to now save for Asmita's marriage. She is no longer a child, as you can see,' said Baba.

'Ah, yes, of course,' responded Ayesha's father, while her mother examined her nails and smiled to herself.

We finally sat down to the elaborate Bengali meal that Ma had put together with Asmita's help. Our guests pecked and sniffed at the food. Ma was visibly upset but played the perfect hostess. There was total silence at the dinner table. I couldn't decide which was more awkward: the lack of conversation or the cross-talk that had taken place in the drawing room.

Finally the evening was over, and goodbyes were said with relief writ large on everbody's face. Ayesha and I went to drop her parents off at the hotel. They invited us up for a drink, but we declined. When we were leaving, they gave me an envelope that contained five thousand rupees – more than a month's salary for me! I protested. Ayesha stepped in and said that it was an old north Indian tradition: the girl's parents had to give some money if they ate at their son-in-law's home. A kind of reimbursement of expenses, I gathered.

When it was time for me to return to Balwanpur, Ayesha offered to stay on for another week with my parents so they would not miss me so much. She squeezed Asmita's and Ma's hands as my car left the driveway of 26 Railway Colony, S.P. Marg. Baba avoided eye contact with me. I could see his eyes were getting moist as I waved from the car.

A year later, Ayesha got her promotion too. Their firm had more trendy designations, so she became Manager, Personnel. We had another round of celebrations. She drove down to Balwanpur and brought a bottle of French wine for Captain Sobti. We went over to his bungalow in the evening and presented it to him. Captain was delighted and very touched.

'Why don't you send a bottle to the old man too?' he suggested. 'Balwan Singh is a connoisseur of wines.'

'I know there is red wine and there is white wine. Red wine with red meat. White wine with white meat. What else is there to know about it?' I enquired.

Ayesha knew, courtesy her father. She said, 'There are table wines and there are cooking wines. My mother uses wine sometimes while cooking western food.'

Captain Sobti lit a cigar and beckoned us to follow him into his study. The room was done up in teakwood, exactly like his office. Inside there were at least two hundred wine bottles stacked in a wooden rack from floor to ceiling. The room was air-conditioned and there was a cupboard containing wine glasses of various shapes and sizes.

Sobti pointed to a set of wine bottles and said, 'To be considered a serious player in corporate India, you need to know your wine. So let me give you a primer. Those bottles there are the table wines, which could be white or red. The dessert wines are generally sweeter. Quite like the equivalent of kheer at the end of a traditional meal. This is a bottle of Port which is a good example of fortified wine. It's extra sweet and has a high alcohol content. And this, of course, is champagne, a sparkling wine which is opened on celebratory occasions such as this. Ayesha beti, you choose a bottle of champagne that we can all share.'

He went on to explain how a different glass was designed for each kind of wine.

We came back home very chirpy. It must have been the champagne that went to our heads.

'I am going to buy a set of wine glasses next month. Now that we are both senior managers, we need to start investing in all this,' I said to Ayesha, who was humming to herself.

'Yeah, no more drinking OM2 from the bucket, like we did at MIJ. My landlord Kevin has some crystal glasses in his apartment. When I come the next time, I'll bring them so we can entertain your colleagues. I'll ask my dad to pick up a bottle of champagne when he goes abroad the next time.'

'Kevin must be a rich bugger to have crystal glasses at home. He hardly spends a week in that apartment. Does he stock Scotch as well? Maybe you could bring some of that along with the glasses. But no, we have the bottle of Chivas that Rusty gifted us. Let's invite Captain Sobti over for dinner tomorrow and we can open the bottle,' I suggested.

'Abbey, we must buy a car now. So many of our batchmates already have. Before we complete our third year at work, we must have a car. Do you know, Kevin has a Mustang in Manhattan. He showed me the pictures when he was here.'

'WHAT? You stayed in the apartment when he was here? You never told me that he was screwing you!' My voice rose in disbelief.

'Abbey! Relax. I saw the pictures in his album. I was out on tour when he was here. I am not sleeping with Kevin, for Christ's sake!'

I came to my senses soon enough, feeling stupid for having jumped to such a hasty conclusion. I made amends the best I could: I went up to Ayesha and held her tight. I whispered a quiet 'sorry' in her ears. And I made it a point to buy a car at the first available opportunity – with money I did not have.

# EIGHT

Another year went by. In June, I got my second promotion and was designated Deputy Manager. Ayesha had been Manager, Personnel for a year already. I used to pretend that I had forgotten to bring my visiting card whenever we were together and she was handing out her business card. But the people at Balwanpur thought I was supremely successful. The other deputy managers had worked for at least ten years before earning the designation. So I was clearly the rising star. Only, I didn't feel like one. I was dying to be called Manager, Personnel.

Mrs Dayal suggested that I avail of a company loan, now that I was Deputy Manager.

'You could buy a nice new Fiat. Better still, a good Ambassador. When you have children you will need a bigger car. Here, try this cake that I made. My daughter Muniya used to love it. She would take it to school every day.'

'I think I'll buy a Maruti. It's almost as good as a Japanese car. I want to be the first person in Balwanpur to drive a Maruti,' I replied as I helped myself to a slice of cake. 'Where is Muniya these days? Why doesn't she ever come here? I have never even met her.'

'She lives with her husband in Jamshedpur. He's a manager in the Iron and Steel Company. The truth is, he doesn't want her to stay in touch with me or visit me. After all, I am just an accounts officer, not good enough to be related to a corporate bigwig's wife. If you ever go to Jamshedpur, let me know. I'll send a cake for Muniya. Anyway, forget all that. Tell me when you are planning to have children. You have been married for so long now. Doesn't Ayesha want to have kids?'

'I think dogs and kids are really cute as long as someone else is looking after them. Neither of us is keen to wake up in the morning just to take a dog for a walk or to change nappies. So we've decided not to have kids. We'll get a car instead. Isn't that a better option?'

Ayesha and I had not had a decent holiday together since our honeymoon in Conoor. Her parents went on an annual holiday to Europe and the way I felt about her family, it became an unspoken agreement between us that Ayesha would accompany her parents. I would always say that I had difficulty getting time off.

I loved travelling, but all my travel so far had been within India. In fact, I could count the number of times I had taken a flight. I would have given my right hand to take a trip abroad.

Ayesha had grown up differently. She had a bunch of relatives in London and the US. She would bring back a bottle of wine and some chocolates from her vacation and I would pass the chocolates on to my parents and tell them that it was a gift from Ayesha.

As things turned out, Ayesha spent all of one week in Balwanpur with me in that whole year. And I could see that a certain coldness had crept into her relationship with my parents and Asmita. I knew exactly what had gone wrong. It had all came spilling out one day when I asked Asmita if she'd met Ayesha recently.

'Ayesha lives so close by and yet never, not once in the last two years, has she invited us to her apartment. She doesn't call us except to wish us Happy Diwali. The other night I heard Baba-Ma saying that she did not even wish them Shubho Bijoya after Durga Puja last year. I met her at Bercos in CP last month, having coffee with her landlord Kevin. She did not even recognize me and even after I waved to her, she just ignored me. I am never going to talk to her again. And you know what, I don't care if she ignores me, I feel awful when she ignores Baba-Ma. I've lost track of the number of times Ma has invited Ayesha home but she always has an excuse for not coming. Baba is hopping mad and says she and her crude clan are not fit to be part of the civilized world, all that they understand is money. Now even Ma has stopped trying to cover up for Ayesha.' Asmita's voice was choked with emotion.

'Don't feel so bad, Asmita. Please. Don't cry. Let me talk to Baba-Ma. I owe them an apology on Ayesha's behalf.' I could feel the anger rising within me as I waited for one of them to come to the phone.

Ma was careful with her words.

'Chotka, when you wanted to marry her, we were convinced that she was not the right person. We felt that she wouldn't understand the family values that you and Asmita have grown up with. Not a single relative of ours was happy either, with the way we were treated by Ayesha's parents at the wedding. But we said, if you are happy, then our opinion does not matter.'

I promised myself that I would not let the relationship drift any further. I would make a genuine attempt to get it back on track. I called up Ayesha and told her to plan a trip to Balwanpur. I had just the surprise for her. It was time to take a loan from the company and buy the car I had promised her.

At the club the other day, I had come across a notice that someone was selling a 'sparingly used' Maruti 800 with 'artificial leather seat covers'. I spoke to Dharminder Satija, the man who could organize anything that money could buy, from a driver's licence to 'genuine Scotch', and even appointments with ministers. For this, we were willing to turn a blind eye to his appearance: his white silk shirts, tight white trousers and matching white patent leather shoes would have put Jeetendra to shame.

'Mysalf Dharminder Satija. Just ji, call me Dharam, like the famous fillum actor from our Punjab – our vary own Dharminder paaji. Mysalf at your service, Sir. You want the latest M'ruti 800? No praablem Sirji. Dharam will get the best car faar you, ji.' He handed me his visiting card. 'I can gat you the bast Scaatch. All genuine drinks only. Not like others who are giving duplicate whisky in original baattle. Captain Sobti just asked me to get one case of Blue Label whisky for the D'rectors' party.'

Dharam Satija could continue ad nauseum about how he knew everyone who mattered, from the Minister of Industries to the local car dealer and mechanic. 'Once you buy car, ji, the mechanic is your best friend,' said Satija, obviously pleased with this insight into life.

Ten days later I was the proud owner of a red-coloured second-hand Maruti 800. I drove to the solitary petrol pump on the outskirts of Balwanpur and introduced myself as a potential customer. The petrol pump attendants looked at each other and smiled and said they were sure they would get to see me frequently.

I took my car for a spin with the windows down. The wind swept my hair into the kind of look that Amitabh Bachchan had made famous. I admired myself in the rearview mirror and wondered how Ayesha would react to this flamboyant husband of hers. I tried driving the car while steering with only my right hand so that I could hold Ayesha's hand with my left. Then for the next mile I practiced lighting my cigarette while driving. This was tough, given the number of stray dogs and cows that the road suddenly sprouted.

I could hardly wait for Ayesha to arrive that weekend. I kept telling her that I had bought her the most expensive gift any man had ever bought for his wife and that she needed to be in Balwanpur to see it for herself. She begged me to tell her what it was but I kept my lips sealed. Half an hour after our call, Ayesha called me back to say she knew what the gift was. It was a solitaire, she guessed. Even better, I teased her. I could picture her delight, how she would cover her mouth and open her eyes wide when she saw the car.

Finally, the much awaited Saturday arrived. I could barely sleep the night before. I had got the house spruced up for her. There were fresh flowers on the table. Mrs Dayal had sent over a freshly baked chocolate cake. I had organized a bottle of white wine that had been chilled and kept in an ice pail I had borrowed from the club's bar. The setting was perfect. I wondered whether I should drive down in my car to the Balwanpur border and let her see the car there, or wait for her to arrive, then show her the car in the garage. I voted in favour of the former. As I reached for the car keys, I noticed for the first time the key chain that Dharam Satija had given me. It was made of wood, and had an 'A' written in brass in the middle. A for Ayesha and A for Abbey, I thought.

I heard a cab pull up outside. Ayesha got out and adjusted her shades, then paid the driver and rang the doorbell. I gave her a big hug and kiss. She always smelt so fresh. I waved the keys in her face.

'Hey, you're early. I was about to set off to meet you en route. But since you're already here, take this. It's for you.'

'Where's my gift? I am dying to see it. I bet it's a solitaire. My mother thought so too. I can read your mind, Abbey.' She sounded so excited that I was not sure what to say.

'Let's go for a drive. We can talk on the way.'

'But Abbey, I just got here!'

And then it dawned on her. 'You mean, you bought a car?'

I laughed with delight and led the way to the garage. Soon we were zipping along the road and out on the highway. I was not sure if Ayesha was immersed in thought or enjoying the ride, she was so silent. 'Aren't you happy with your gift?' I asked.

Before she could answer, the car sputtered and stopped in the middle of the highway. The heat outside was unbearable. I opened the bonnet and peered in to see what had gone wrong but everything seemed okay, except that the car would not start. The battery had probably gone dead. I asked Ayesha to push the car so I could jumpstart it. She refused. There was absolutely no traffic on the road. The nearest spot of civilization was probably the petrol pump, which was a good twenty-minute walk away. Ayesha would not go with me, and though it was unsafe to leave her there alone, I had no choice but to look for a mechanic.

The mechanic at the petrol pump almost seemed to be expecting me. He told me that the car's previous owner had brought it in with major mechanical problems. Then he had invested some money in painting and polishing the car, fitted it with fake leather seats and sold it off to me. It had some fundamental problems that would never go away. Sell it off to someone else, the mechanic suggested. I felt cheated, my faith in the world shaken. Why hadn't the bastard Dharam Satija warned me? Now here I was, saddled with a loan that I would take ten years to pay off for a car that I could not even drive.

The car was eventually repaired temporarily so I could drive it back home. The moment we reached, Ayesha locked herself in the bedroom and cried loudly. In the evening she opened the door and said that she wanted to talk to me. I had a lot of things to tell her as well. And none of it was pleasant.

'Abbey, I don't think our marriage is working out. You are a typical middle-class Bong whose high point in life is to buy a second-hand Maruti 800. Even then, you are one of the last among our classmates to buy a car. You call to tell me that you have bought a gift for ME. And what is my gift? A SECOND-HAND fucking car that you bought to drive yourself to office. You are a selfish loser, that's what you are, Abbey.'

'That's a bloody lie. I did buy the car for you. Not because I needed one. I walk to the office anyway. I bought the car because it was so important to you. You keep comparing your husband with everyone else – with every classmate of ours, with the neighbours, and with you. No matter who you compare me with, I always fall short. How do you think I feel? And the way you have behaved with Baba-Ma and Asmita is disgusting. They feel ignored and humiliated.'

'You haven't had much to do with my parents either.' Ayesha was shrieking by now. I was afraid Mrs Dayal could hear us.

'Don't fucking shout, Ayesha. Your parents have not been civil with me either. Have they even spoken to me? Oh yes, I should not forget the five whole minutes of conversation they had with me during the wedding. As far as they are concerned, I am a mistake their darling daughter has made. You continue with your European holidays and discussing wine and cheese with your parents. But you don't have the civility to call up my parents, leave alone visit them. Not once during the last two years have you found the time to meet them, though you live barely twenty minutes away. Baba-Ma are hurt. Very hurt.'

'I married you, Abbey. I didn't marry your family. All your parents do is talk about you and your sister. I hate everything about you and your family. You Bengalis are the world's most pretentious lot.'

'Ha! And you and your Punjabi clan, let me tell you, are the gold standard of crudeness. Have you noticed how your entire clan gets withdrawal symptoms if they don't get their alcohol by 7 p.m.? Fuck, you guys are a desperate lot.'

The next morning Ayesha got up early and left. I did not go to the door to see her off. When I sat down at the dining table, I saw the sheet of paper with her writing on it, fluttering under an empty coffee mug.

Abbey,

Every woman wants to marry someone who she can wake up to and snuggle up to, without worrying about looking pretty. Like all girls of my age, I too dreamt that I would find that someone special whose eyes could warm a cold winter night. Who would buy me flowers and chocolates and kiss my cheeks for no reason. You were never that person for me. Not that you were incapable, just plain unwilling.

I have seen you be such a person, Abbey – not with me, but with Keya. I saw the two of you walking in the pouring rain, pretending that it wasn't even getting your clothes wet. I thought you would be the same to me, but I was wrong. I even tried to be nice to your parents and sister because I knew they mattered to you. But not once did you care for my parents. You were always so judgmental about their ways. Is it their fault that they are rich and yours are not? The Abbey I loved had a sense of humour and was a diehard romantic. But you only care about your work and yourself and your parents and your sister. In all the time that we stayed apart, not once did you tell me that you love me and that you missed me. For you I will always remain a trophy that you snatched from others without even trying. Other than sex, I am not even sure what you want from me.

I hate you for having ruined my life. I will not let you do it any longer. You can stay in this foxhole called Balwanpur. I am off to explore the rest of the world with Kevin.

Ayesha

As I stood there with the letter in my hand, I asked myself what I was feeling. The answer was not what it ought to have been. I ought to have been heart-broken. But I wasn't. I felt relieved and cheated, and used and misunderstood. Ayesha was out of my life and in Kevin's. And all I could feel was an enormous sense of relief, that it was finally over.

In the evening Mrs Dayal sent me a note asking whether she should send food for two. She had obviously seen Ayesha drive away in the cab early in the morning. So what was the point of asking me? Maybe I should just knock on her door and announce it myself. 'My wife is off with Kevin. Henceforth and forever, please send me one serving only. Thank you.'

I poured myself some OM2 and lit a cigarette. The lights were off. I put on some music but there was no respite. Everyone wanted to know the gossip about me, even Pink Floyd. The lyrics of 'Comfortably Numb' echoed in my head:

Is there anybody in there?
Just nod if you can hear me.
Is there anyone home?

Come on, now.
I hear you're feeling down.
Well I can ease your pain,
Get you on your feet again.
Relax.
I need some information first.
Just the basic facts:
Can you show me where it hurts?

# NINE

I could not bear to go to the office the next morning. I called up Captain Sobti and told him I was feeling unwell. This was the first time in three years that I had called in sick. Captain Sobti just said 'Hmm' and disconnected the phone. I didn't have the heart to see Dr Patronobish and endure his line of questioning, either. It was always difficult to figure out whether he wanted to know something that would impact the patient's treatment or whether it was idle curiosity. So I called back Captain Sobti and told him it was nothing serious. Just a mild headache, I said. Sobti did not probe.

I lay in bed and spent the day alternately sulking and smoking.

*Should I take a few days' leave and go off by myself to a hill station?*

*How will you explain this juicy piece of gossip to your colleagues and everyone else? They'll get to know sooner rather than later.*

*Maybe I should just return the sewing machine to*

*Sohanlal Negi. Anyway, what had made them think Ayesha
would use it to sew my shirts?*

*Should I kill Dharam Satija for ruining my marriage?
Or thank him?*

*How will I explain it to Baba and Ma? Nobody in our
family has been through a divorce.*

*Technically, you are still married to Ayesha. It's just
that she is living with Kevin. And you are by yourself. That's
humiliating.*

*The solution for everything is not Old Monk. Go for a
run – not rum.*

Through the daze I was in, I realized that the doorbell
had been ringing for a while. Who the hell could it be? I
hoped it wasn't Pat or Sobti, and that I looked suitably
sick. Having a day old stubble helped.

It was Negi at the door. That was quick. Ayesha had
barely left me and already he wanted the wedding gift
back?

'I have been looking all over the place for you, sahib.
There is a big problem in the workers' canteen. When
they were serving lunch for the first shift workers, someone
found a cockroach in the rice. The workers are angry and
say that they will not eat until fresh rice is cooked for
them and until then they will not work either.'

'Who found the cockroach? How do we know he didn't
put it there on purpose?' I asked as I changed into my
work clothes and started to walk towards the canteen.

Sohanlal kept talking as he kept pace with me. 'You
are absolutely right, sahib, it is that leader of the Irula

gang – Arai. He must have done it on purpose. His people catch all kinds of dirty animals and snakes. He has been calling the Irula workers together and trying to form a separate union. Arai tells them that our union is on the payrolls of the management and hence can never do anything for the workers' benefit. We should find a way to file a false charge of theft or something against Arai and terminate his services.' I'd had no clue that Sohanlal was such a scheming sod. Looks were indeed deceptive.

The workers' canteen was buzzing. The men had gathered around and some were obviously using the opportunity to wrangle time off. I spoke to the first group that I met outside. They repeated the facts for me. The kitchen workers were standing around looking scared. They were afraid they would be lynched if they faced the mob. They told me it would take four hours to cook the same amount of rice again and it would disrupt the service for the other shifts.

Negi saw my predicament and whispered in my ears, 'Tell them you will pay them cash in lieu of the food. That should ensure that the next shift is not affected.'

'What happens if someone else discovers a cockroach? We will then continue to pay everyone for their meals and end up running a subsidized canteen. Are you mad?' I asked Sohanlal. 'You should tell the workers that according to the law, we have the right to deduct money from them as per the principle of "no work, no pay". I should ask our legal department whether we can do it right away. That will discourage them from using a silly excuse to stop work.'

'You want to face a hungry, angry mob instead? You never know what they might do to you.' Sohanlal Negi did not seem like a nice guy any more.

'The mob will do nothing. Abbey, let's go in now and face them.' I jumped on hearing the voice of Captain Sobti, who had quietly appeared on the scene.

He was in his usual black shirt and trousers with a leather bag slung over his shoulders. Only I knew that it contained his cigars. Everyone else believed that he carried a revolver.

The workers made way for us as we entered. We walked up to the table where Arai sat with a plate of rice in front of him. The cockroach was visible and Arai was guarding it as though it was a piece of evidence to be produced in a court of law.

'This is what they cook for us. The workers don't even get a hygienically cooked meal in this company. Would they dare to do this in the managers' cafeteria?' Arai spoke in his heavily accented Hindi.

'Let me see what you are talking about, Arai. Give me the plate of rice. Hmm... it happens to all of us, even at home. Right?' said Captain Sobti to the mob that had begun to tighten around us. 'What do we do when it happens at home? We just pick up the cockroach, throw it away, wipe the plate and continue with our meal. I am so hungry. Will someone serve me some good hot sambar?'

Captain Sobti ate the rice and sambar with relish and Arai, for want of anything else to do, resumed his lunch. I too sat down and ate. Captain Sobti and Arai soon started talking about other things. Arai's son Daya wanted to be a sportsman. Captain Sobti recommended that Daya take up athletics.

'Daya won the 100-metre dash at the sports day last year. This year you should coach him to improve his timing. Let him practice early in the morning. I have a friend whose son left behind a great pair of running shoes. Daya can borrow those. Or keep them if they fit him.' Sobti had a way of reaching out to people.

'You are really kind. Daya has been pestering me for a new pair. I told him that he is only ten years old and does not need shoes. He can practice running barefoot. He does not have to depend on shoes to improve his performance.' Arai looked at Sobti for support.

'Running barefoot while doing the warm-up is fine. The contact with the earth will tell him whether he is landing too hard or in the wrong spot. The best shoes are those that make you feel like you are running barefoot. Ask him to try this new pair. And now let me get back to work, I have a meeting in fifteen minutes.' Sobti got up and left.

I went back to the office as if on autopilot. It occurred to me that I had called up Sobti and told him just a little while ago that I was unwell. I should not have eaten the sambar rice at the canteen. He would never believe my excuse now.

'Glad you are feeling better, Abbey. I was expecting you,' said Captain Sobti as soon as I entered.

'I am feeling much better now, Captain. Might as well get some work done.' I spat out the reason.

'It's never easy when someone leaves you. If that someone happens to be your wife, it hurts much more. You haven't been married that long. Which means it's the humiliation that's hard to deal with, even more than the rejection itself.' Sobti said all this without making eye contact.

He sat there smoking his cigar while I subtly wiped away the traitor of a teardrop that had appeared for no good reason. I was grateful for the cigar smoke that lay thick in the room.

'Deal with it head on, Abbey. When you find someone fishing for gossip, just be upfront and say you decided to part ways amicably. That will put an end to the speculation after a few days. Public memory is so short. And thank God for that.'

I couldn't help the outburst that followed: 'I hate living in a fishbowl like this. I am sure everyone in Balwanpur already knows that Ayesha has left me. There is no sense of privacy at all. I hate this place.'

'We are all part of some fishbowl or the other. When you were at MIJ you were part of that fish tank. Before that you were part of the fish in a tank called SRCC or Delhi University, right? The tank has changed in shape and size but you remain part of one. It's just that this one is called Balwanpur.'

I accepted Captain Sobti's invitation to dinner that evening. He met me at the door, wearing a colourful shirt and a pair of jeans. He poured me a large cocktail, which he called a Daiquiri.

'It was known to be Ernest Hemingway's favourite drink. A large peg of light rum, two tablespoons of freshly squeezed lime juice and a tablespoon of sugar syrup. Before you pour the drink you need to fill the glass with crushed ice and add a slice of lime to it.'

'Cheers, Captain And thanks for stepping in this morning. I would have taken the legal route and caused a disaster.'

Captain Sobti lit his cigar and said, 'You need to build your bridges with the Irulas. They will continue to be a force to reckon with long after I am gone. The man to watch is Arai. He is incorruptible and has the welfare of the workers at heart. Sohanlal is a spent force. All he understands is money. Make sure you spend time talking to the Irulas. They must see you as the new generation leader among the managers. And remember, Abbey, the law exists as a fall back option only when all communication between human beings has failed. Don't be in a hurry to use the law instead of dialogue. Personnel managers, or human resource managers, as the newspapers call them these days, need to build a direct bond with the employees in order to be successful. By that, I don't mean HR managers have to be touchy-feely. That helps, but it is not a substitute for building business knowledge.'

'I would agree that Arai is the person to watch. He seems to have the support of most employees, not just the Irulas. To think that I almost ruined my relationship with him even before it began!'

'Look for an opportunity to make him a hero. That's the best way to build your rapport with Arai. Also, his son Daya may well be the next big thing in athletics. He is such an amazing runner. I want to give him a sports scholarship on behalf of the company.'

'I could visit him at home. Maybe I should carry the sneakers for his son,' I suggested

'Don't make it look like you are bending over backwards to please him. That will upset the power equation. Call him to the office and give him the shoes. Find some other opportunity to reward him and make sure your incentive rewards the right behaviour,' Captain Sobti said.

'Do you remember reading about the scientist Pavlov's experiment? His dog's reaction was to salivate every time he heard Pavlov ringing the bell. That's because Pavlov had conditioned it by ringing the bell every time he served food to the dog. Thereafter, even when there was no food, the dog would salivate at the sound of the bell.

'Every HR manager has the ability to impact employee behaviour through the system of incentives. Spend time understanding how incentives impact human behaviour. Every promotion decision of the company does more to impact the culture of an organization than any poster or vision statement. Managers always need to ask if they are rewarding someone for the right reasons.'

'So if we want to discourage absenteeism among the workers, we should reward people who show up for work regularly, right?'

'Do that only if you wish to reward someone just for showing up for work. For all you know, people will expect a separate incentive to work, after they've shown up. I know you will say we should punish people who don't work. That is an example of a negative incentive.

'One day you will be leading the HR function of this company. So let me tell you a few things today that you must keep in mind. In any organization, you can reach the middle management level based on pure merit. But beyond that, many other factors – most of which you are not in control of – come into effect. Collectively speaking, these traits can be called Organizational Smartness. You will often hear people say, let your work speak for itself. The work does not speak, people do. The people who make career decisions about you need to have the appropriate information. If you do not tell them, how will they decide in your favour? Yet, this is against our basic culture.'

'So how do I become Org Smart?'

'Lesson number one is what the Godfather said long ago – "Keep your friends close but your enemies closer." The English language uses different words for friend and colleague. They are meant to be different. You can be close to your colleagues but don't expect them to be your friends. Lesson number two – manage the way others perceive you. Corollary: If life is a stage, remember to dress appropriately to render the character believable. It impacts perceptions about credibility and competence that people will have about you. Remember, I said that it impacts perceptions. So while you need to be competent and work hard, who you play golf with may decide which housing complex you live in! The biggest Org Smart tip I can give you is to make sure your boss has heard and agreed with your point of view before you go public with it. The Americans have an interesting term for it – it is called aligning the boss. So the "meeting before the meeting" helps you to align all those stakeholders who will need to support your decision during the meeting.'

The cigar had reduced itself to a lump. Captain Sobti got up to pour himself another drink and continued, 'I think you are smart, you work hard and you are ambitious. I am going to now expect you to start doing things on your own and not just implement what I have designed. You need to help the workers' union through a transition. Negi needs to go; Arai needs to take over. Go figure out how to make that happen.'

When I got back home I was a little dizzy with all that alcohol inside me. I lit a cigarette and thought of all that Captain Sobti had told me. And all the time, buried just beneath, was a feeling that kept rearing its head like the Lochness Monster. Missing Ayesha. I missed her. I missed her sense of humour. I missed picking up the phone to her and discussing all that Captain and I had just talked about. I thought of all the good times we had had together. The mornings in Conoor when we sat and drank coffee. That spot on the planet belonged to Ayesha and me. I

arm. He had its head firmly in his hand, so no matter how hard the snake wriggled, Arai was safe. I saw this as a godsent opportunity to build my rapport with the man.

'Where did you find that snake, Arai? I thought Balwanpur was snake free. This is the first time I have seen one since I joined.'

'There are plenty of snakes around here but you don't see them. That is because the Irulas risk their lives to catch them and keep the employees safe and yet, after working for so many years we have not been made to feel a part of the company. After so many years, we are still working as temporary workers. We have come a long way from home in search of a livelihood. We want to be on the permanent rolls of the company and not on the rolls of some contractor who uses Irulas to mow the lawns and keep the gardens snake free. We get no benefits. We cannot live in the houses in the Workers' Colony, we have to live on the outskirts of the township in dingy huts. Last year alone, four Irulas died of snake bite and they received no compensation, nor were their sons provided employment in the company. Can you truthfully say we have been treated fairly?'

I could see the situation was quickly turning into a no-win scenario for us. I remembered Captain Sobti's lesson: 'Never negotiate with a mob.' I thought quickly and asked Arai to request the others to leave.

Arai used the chance to make another speech. He said, 'They will leave. They are hard-working people. Promise me, sir, that you will give us a patient hearing.'

'I will. Send that snake back with one of your friends and come into the office. I have something for you.'

Somebody stepped up to Arai and held open a brown sack. In a flash Arai dropped the hissing cobra in and shut the bag tight. Then he passed it to a young kid who stood beside him, a mute spectator to the drama, and said, 'Daya, take it home and give it to Amma. She will know what to do. I don't want to see you playing with this one.'

Arai walked into the office and looked at me curiously. I went to the cash-box and counted out five thousand rupees.

'This is for you, Arai. For catching a King Cobra. This is your reward.'

'I will not take anything for myself. But I will distribute it among the two hundred Irula families that live on the borderline of starvation. Thank you, sir. Thank you for rewarding us. The next time you are driving to Delhi, please visit us.' Arai got up and shook my hand.

Compared to Sohanlal Negi and so many of the workers I had met, Arai was different. His body language was unusual. He looked everyone straight in the eye and spoke in a way that made it clear that he was only demanding his due and not a favour. I secretly liked the guy's attitude. It was evident that Arai was a future leader. I was pleased at my decision to give him money but also impressed that he had not taken it for himself but for his people.

That week, two more Irulas brought in snakes. I gave them fifty rupees each. The following week a total of ten snakes were brought in. I wondered if they were the same ones being brought in everyday. So I got the men to leave the snakes in an old glass aquarium that was lying in the office.

The week after, there were twenty-eight snakes. This was getting crazy. I set up a counter for an hour in the afternoon when snakes could be brought in. I also prepared a rate card. We would now pay twenty rupees a snake, provided it was a poisonous species. Captain Sobti was very uncomfortable with the idea of handing out money each time a snake was brought in, and with their being dumped in the aquarium. He was afraid the snakes would escape. So we put two of our security guards on duty to make sure such a thing did not happen. The week after, when sixty-four snakes were brought in, including some that were clearly babies, I realized there was a problem. I would have to visit the Irula village to find out what was going on.

The village was on the outskirts of the township. Half-naked children were playing with snakes under a tree. They seemed as comfortable touching the snakes as I would be playing with a puppy. I met Arai, who was talking to a few men bunched around him. They were listening to him with rapt attention. Occasionally one of them would break into rapid speech, gesticulating and pointing at a well nearby. I couldn't understand what they were arguing about as they were speaking Tamil. My knowledge of the language was limited to synonyms for fornication and some parts of the male anatomy –

and I swear I heard some references to those too. They saw me and went away, leaving Arai to face me. I peeked into the well and withdrew in horror. It was a snake pit with hundreds of baby snakes.

'So now I know where those snakes are coming from. You are breeding snakes. That's a clever way to make money, Arai.' I had to try very hard to keep my voice from rising.

'The first day you paid us five thousand for one snake. Now you have made the rate twenty rupees. So the boys have had to breed snakes to get more money,' Arai said softly.

'You must think I am crazy. The scheme is withdrawn. No more money for bringing in poisonous snakes. You can tell everyone that. Tomorrow morning I will send back all the snakes we have in the aquarium near the office. You can do what you want with them.' I walked off in a huff.

As soon as Arai made the announcement, a loud protest went up. But I had to show them who was boss. When I went back and told Captain Sobti what had happened, he rolled his eyes in horror and said that the scheme had been a mistake to start with.

'Think, Abbey, think. What sort of behaviour did you incentivize? You rewarded him for bringing in a poisonous snake. Five thousand rupees is nearly a year's salary for a worker. You showed them an easy way to make money. You even created a formal process around it. Then you lowered the amount you paid for each snake.

So they had to breed more snakes to make the same amount of money. Now that you have withdrawn the scheme, they will just release all those snakes into the wild. Oh my God! You have destroyed the safety of this place in three weeks. This is really unforgivable. You will receive no increment this year.' Captain Sobti added the last bit as he walked off.

That wasn't fair. He made the whole thing sound like a mega act of stupidity. Now I would never be considered for promotion to manager. Suddenly, I hated Sobti with all my heart. He was a stupid old fool who had outlived his stay in the company. That night, before going to bed, I prayed sincerely to God that he would get Sobti out of my way. As an afterthought, I left the choice of methodology to God. After all, there were many ways in which the task could be accomplished.

# ELEVEN

I had to make a trip to Delhi. It was a month since Ayesha had left Balwanpur, and I felt a lot more comfortable with the idea of our living apart. Now I had to break the news of my failed marriage to my family. They had not explicitly asked me if something was wrong, so I had not told them, either. Sometimes I had caught myself wishing Ayesha would come back so that I would be saved the hassle of breaking the news at home. I wondered how my batchmates would react. I made a mental note to avoid all the places where I might meet them.

I felt a sense of shame deep inside me. I was a failure. I had thought that I had finally learnt the art of building relationships after I married Ayesha. Her walking away seemed like a report card on my abilities. It may sound funny, but I swear people gave me curious looks and I was sure that everyone in the township was talking about Ayesha's walking out on me. I hated living in Balwanpur. Everyone here was on display all the time. Maybe I should get myself a transfer to Delhi. But even that didn't seem so easy.

*Will Captain Sobti find you an assignment in the Head Office just because Ayesha has run away and you are not man enough to face the people in the township?*

*I should ask for a change. I want to do something different. I have had enough of this role of handling workers.*

*If you went to Delhi, you would have to stay at home, and that would mean explaining to the people in the colony as well. Even if you managed to avoid the questions, your parents and sister would not be spared.*

I thought of leaving my job. But there was no privacy here. How could I even receive a call for an interview without the whole township knowing the details? All our letters were routinely delivered to a post box in Delhi and then brought here. I kicked myself for having moved to the boondocks for my first job. The only option now was to find something in Delhi.

I told Captain Sobti that I needed to get a different job, maybe as part of the Corporate Support Team in Balwan Singh's office in Delhi. He was not amused and told me that it was too soon to look for a new assignment.

'You are getting ready to take over the role of personnel manager in the factory. Why do you want to walk away from it? Don't let that comment about no increment this year demoralize you. That was said in a fit of anger. You know I don't mean it.' Captain Sobti stood erect as he faced me, as if he was commanding a platoon of bombers.

I just dug the heel of my shoe into the carpet in his office and looked at my shoelaces intently.

Captain Sobti looked quietly at me, then relented. 'Very well then, you should go and spend a week in Delhi and let Mr Balwan Singh decide if he needs you in his team. Good luck. I will miss you.'

I wanted to jump in joy. But I restrained myself and left his office quietly. I walked back to the house that evening and poured myself a large OM2. I put my feet up and listened to my favourite album – Kishore Kumar singing songs written by Gulzar and set to music by R.D. Burman.

The next Sunday I drove into Delhi, feeling triumphant and nervous at the same time. I checked into the Taj, showered, and was about to take a walk down to meet my friends at the Railway Club when I noticed someone had slipped a note under the door.

'If you are free, can I drop in – K.'

This was just what I needed – sympathy from that idiot, Kevin. First he ran off with my wife. Then he wanted to tell me why Ayesha had been miserable with me and how he had actually helped us both. I called him some choice names in my head and decided to ignore him. How the hell did that bimbo-hunter know I was staying at this hotel, anyway? I opened the door and nearly walked into someone who was standing at my door. It was Keya. She stood there in a blue silk saree that made her look ravishing. But it also made her look like one of the girls at the front office of the hotel. Her hair fell free to her shoulders, not in two plaits, the way it used to be when I first saw her at MIJ.

'You've changed your hairstyle, Keya. You don't do it in two plaits any more?'

'The only person who can pull that off at any age is Lata Mangeshkar. Hi, are you in a hurry to go somewhere?' said Keya softly, with a smile. The sparkle in her kohl-rimmed eyes was still the same.

'Of course not. I was just planning to walk down to the Railway Club and see if I could find someone familiar. Come on in. You look like one of the girls in the lobby. Do you know, this is the first time I've seen you in a saree. I swear you look pretty. But wait, we'd better go somewhere else and chat. Someone might be coming to look for me in the room.' I handed her Kevin's note.

'That's my note, Abbey. I wanted to see you when I got to know that you were staying on our property. I am wearing this saree because I am one of the girls from the hotel's sales team.' Keya sat down by the side of the bed. I could only stand there and look at her in disbelief.

'So when Ayesha met my parents in the hotel, it was you and not Kevin who sent the chocolate cake? It was you, not Kevin, who sent the bouquet of pink gladioli to my room with the box of Godiva chocolates and that lovely card that said "Wishing you and Ayesha the very best – K"?'

'You forgot the red roses I sent to you and Ayesha on your wedding night, with a note. I thought that was a clever line: Sure you will be happy ToGetHer'. Keya laughed, her usual infectious laugh.

My head was spinning. All the while, Keya had been

sending me SOS messages and I had thought they were from Kevin. I felt giddy and had to sit down. My head was throbbing. She brought me a glass of water and splashed some on my face.

'Are you okay, Abbey?'

'Keya, why the hell didn't you meet me when you came to Delhi? I wrote to you twice after I came here. You never replied to me. Do you know I married Ayesha?'

She had not lost her sense of humour. 'Of course I know, Abbey. I just told you about the card.'

'You knew I was here and yet you didn't contact me! That's a crime, Keya. Life could have been so different. Would you like something to drink? I need a strong cappuccino.' I picked up the phone to call room service and ordered two when Keya nodded.

'It's called destiny, Abbey. How else can you explain my getting late on the day you were leaving MIJ? A large truck with a broken axle blocked the traffic on the road to the station. We were stuck behind a long line of vehicles, crawling along in single file. I was desperate to meet you. I got out of the car and ran to the station. By the time I located your compartment, the train was leaving the station. I kept shouting that I was coming to Delhi in August.'

'Yes, I heard you say that you were coming to Delhi in August. Why did you not get in touch with me then? I waited for you and then lost all hope. Believe me, Keya. I wrote to you twice after I reached Delhi.'

'My uncle had retired and we moved out of the house

near Bijli Park to another house near the Subarnarekha. This was shortly after we broke up, so you didn't have the latest address. Does that explain why I never got your letters?'

'Keya, this is crazy. You should have met me when you came to Delhi. Ayesha knew where I lived.'

'I was in touch with Ayesha all the time. She told me how deeply in love you two were. She told me about how you and she got drunk and had sex on the last night of the summer training. I couldn't take that, Abbey.'

I could have killed Ayesha. 'So it was Ayesha who tattled. I always assumed Gopher had sneaked. Gosh! I never knew she was such a manipulative bitch. I hate her. I hate Ayesha.'

Keya continued, 'I never expected that she would actually invite me to stay with her when I came to Delhi for the job interview at the hotel. Even though we were classmates in school, you know I could never stand her catty behaviour. She was always so weird, even then. Every time one of the girls in our class had a crush on a guy, she would go after him and flirt with him till he started chasing her instead. Then she would lose all interest in him. She hasn't had a single steady relationship in her life.'

'Yeah, Ayesha can be a real bitch.' I couldn't help but vent, though she was still my wife and I owed her silence at the very least.

'I can never forget that evening. I had got my job offer from the Taj. I was so thrilled. I asked Ayesha for your address. I wanted to drop in and give you a surprise. She told me that you had proposed to her and had invited her to meet your parents for dinner that evening. At first, I didn't believe her. Then I peeped into the restaurant and saw her talking to your parents and sister. That's when I realized that you and Ayesha were indeed getting married to each other. So I went to the Cake Shoppe and sent you the chocolate cake and that note. I thought you would ask for me after seeing the note. I was wrong. You didn't even make an effort to find out where I was.' Keya was sobbing now.

'Keya, please believe me. I did not propose to Ayesha that evening. She just dropped into the restaurant with her landlord Kevin and happened to meet my parents. If she told you otherwise, she was lying. I swear, Keya, I thought the cake was from Kevin because the card said "With compliments from K". How could I have guessed that you would be so cryptic?'

'Abbey, did you really believe that Kevin sent you pink flowers and chocolates? Is he gay? I can tell you he isn't! If Ayesha is to be believed, he bought her diamonds every month when he stayed with her in Delhi.' Keya was playing with the single silver toe-ring that she wore on her right foot.

'What! Ayesha told me that Kevin was in India once a year for a week. I didn't know he came every month. No wonder he let her stay there. I hate Ayesha. After taking me away from you, she just carried on with her life. I could kill her for her selfishness. You should see the letter she left for me when she walked out. She wrote a big thesis on how I had ruined her life.' I kicked the carpet in disgust.

There was a knock on the door. It was the waiter, with our cappuccino. We sat and sipped in silence. Keya doodled on the writing pad on the table by the bed. I sat and smoked two cigarettes and only then realized that she was crying.

I got up and sat next to her and held her tight. I wanted to cry too, but the overwhelming feeling was of anger, at Ayesha, at myself, and a sense of despair at what might have been. Gently, I dried Keya's tears, and then it happened. I kissed her eyes. I could taste the salty tears as I kissed her cheeks and then slowly and deliberately, I kissed her on the lips.

'I love you, Keya. I always have. I am sorry for what I've done to us.'

'I love you too. Don't leave me again, Abbey,' Keya said, her lips soft and yielding under my mouth.

We turned off the light in the room. When I woke up in the morning she had left. The note pad on which she had doodled was still there to tell me that the evening had been for real.

# Twelve

I told Baba and Ma about Ayesha. They were shocked but not surprised. Asmita told me that there had been plenty of gossip, with half the world having seen Ayesha and Kevin together. The day she met them at a restaurant in CP, she had known there was something wrong. Asmita told me that Kevin was holding Ayesha's hand and hugging her every now and then.

'You should get a divorce. Maybe you should get married again. We will find a nice girl for you, Bhai. Ayesha wasn't right for you. She has only made everyone unhappy. You deserve better.' My kid sister sounded wise beyond her years.

'Now it's your turn to get married. You are in the first year of your MA. Time for us to start looking for a match – unless you plan to make life easier for us.'

'Bhai, you know I want to work after college. I want to be financially independent before I marry. And guess what, you'll be unmarried too soon, just like me!' She skipped out of reach as I tried to yank her pigtails.

I went to meet Balwan Singh in his office on Barakhamba Road the next day. He had asked me to come at 3 p.m. The office was luxuriously furnished. There was a pretty woman in a short skirt who was polishing her nails and receiving calls at the reception.

At 3 p.m. I was escorted into Balwan Singh's office by another NN (Nubile Nymphet, in other words) in a white blouse and smart black skirt. Tiny silver earrings swung from her dainty earlobes. All the girls here seemed to be in uniform.

'Captain Sobti tells me that you want to join my strategic taskforce. He spoke very highly of you and I trust his judgment. I could certainly find plenty for you to do. This company needs to see major changes in its people strategy. Let me warn you, though, I am a difficult person to deal with. In my team we work hard and play hard, but never at the same time.

'Go and call Tinasha for me. I'll have her organize a desk for you, and find a place for you to stay. You need to be within a five-minute walk of the office so that you don't waste time travelling. Remember, your time is my time now. So take a few days off. From the first of October, you'll be part of my team. '

I stepped out and asked for Tinasha. She turned out to be the NN with the silver earrings. She walked into Balwan Singh's office and emerged ten minutes later with a broad smile.

'Welcome to our team, Abbey. I am Tinasha. People here call me Nasha.'

'How did you get that name?'

'My parents named me Asha. I preferred the name Tina for myself. When I went to school I told them my name was Tina-Asha and the name stuck. In the office it's got shortened to Nasha.'

'Nasha… does that mean addiction or intoxication?' I asked her with a smile.

'Once you get intoxicated, addiction is easy.' She smiled back.

I was given a lovely desk with a window that overlooked Barakhamba Road and the hustle and bustle of the city. I was also given a beautiful apartment that was tastefully done up. It was better than any I had seen in Balwanpur. I asked Nasha what rules applied to me.

'You are now part of the Chairman's office. You take what you need. There are no rules. You live in style and you will travel in style. You represent the Chairman of Balwanpur Industries. Make sure you are in the office by 10 a.m. every day. Also, I noticed that you call him Mr Balwan Singh. That's not on. He likes to be called BS or Mr Singh. Oh, and there's a dress code. Men can wear only black trousers and white shirts. No cufflinks. You must always look perfectly groomed. At night you leave the office only after BS has left. Have you met the others in his group?' Nasha enquired.

I met the others. There was Rohan Chandra, an MBA from an Ivy League college in the US, who had a pronounced American accent.

'Hi, I am Rohan. I look after S&M in the office. That

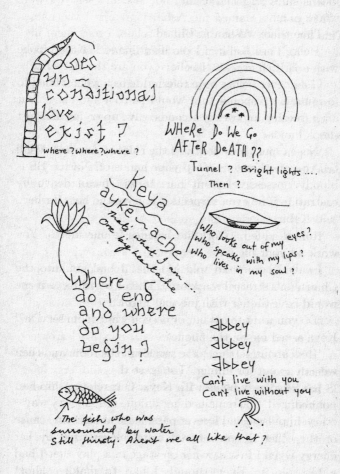

Does un~ conditional love exist ?

where ? where ? where ?

WHeRe Do We Go AFTeR DeATH ??

Tunnel ? Bright lights ....

Then ?

Keya ayke ~ ache thats what I am ... One big heartache

who looks out of my eyes? who speaks with my lips? Who lives in my soul ?

Where do I end and where do you begin ?

Abbey
Abbey
Abbey

Can't live with you
Can't live without you

The fish who was surrounded by water Still thirsty. Aren't we all like that ?

means sales and marketing, not sex, in case you were wondering.'

Then there was Kabir Bijlani.

'Hello, I am Kabir. I look after finance.' Kabir spoke with a British accent. 'I believe you are the HR whiz.'

I had never before been referred to as a whiz. I tried to formulate a response that would be cool and clever but after freezing for twenty seconds, gave up trying and just shook hands.

'Nasha must have told you the rules of the road. We'll tell you another one. Keep your hands off Nasha. BS is bloody possessive about her. It will mean death by castration if he even suspects you have the hots for her,' said Kabir.

Rohan added, 'Work-life balance is our motto. You work all your life.'

I called home and told Ma that I had got into the Chairman's strategic taskforce. Then I asked Keya if she would have dinner with me that night.

'Do you want to eat out or do you want room service?' Keya asked me on the phone.

'How about getting some service in the room and then we can go out for dinner,' I suggested.

It was so easy being with Keya. Our relationship had not changed. She remained her unique self in every way – crazy, impulsive and forever passionate about some cause or the other. I remembered being mesmerized by her energy when I first saw her on stage in a play that I had a bit role in. Even though I had to make a short appearance in Act III, I would be at rehearsal from Act I Scene 1, to make sure I didn't miss a single hundred-watt smile of hers. I loved Keya's smile. I loved all of her.

'Abbey, will you write a poem for me? On my body. Use this pen. Someday I may get it tattooed, what do you think? Oh, stop staring at me like that. Haven't you seen a naked woman before?'

Obediently, I took the black-ink pen from her hand and started to write the words she murmured to me almost absentmindedly:

> I want you to know
> one thing.

> You know how this is:
> if I look
> at the crystal moon, at the red branch
> of the slow autumn at my window,
> if I touch
> near the fire
> the impalpable ash
> or the wrinkled body of the log,
> everything carries me to you,
> as if everything that exists,
> aromas, light, metals,
> were little boats
> that sail
> toward those isles of yours that wait for me.

Keya was asleep by the time I finished adding my illustrations to the words. It was quite late when I fell asleep, my body spooned into hers. When the morning sun woke me, I lay quietly, looking at her sleeping next to me on the snow-white sheets with those words in black glistening against her fair skin. I kissed her eyes lightly and turned over on my stomach to watch her sleep. I could have looked at her forever.

# THIRTEEN

Life was a mad buzz in the corporate office. Balwan Singh was a workaholic. He started his day at 5.30 a.m. with three hours on the golf course, and followed that up with an hour in his apartment, planning his schedule for the day with Nasha. The rest of the day depended on how well Nasha had managed to anticipate his questions and needs. She would systematically write out his appointments and label them with colour-coded stickies. His train or air tickets had to be put in a folder with a copy of the day's plan and a 3x5 index card that had a brief profile of the people he was meeting that day. After each meeting we would go into his office and update the index cards based on his notes and comments. I was amazed at how much he accomplished in a day. Every appointment in his calendar had one line on 'objective to be accomplished'. There were no open-ended conversations with BS.

A week after I had joined, he abruptly asked me, 'What have you observed about my working habits?'

'The way you manage time is admirable. Your ability to get the most out of the same twenty-four hours that everyone else has is amazing,' I said to him in a tone that did not hide my awe.

'No one manages time. You manage yourself to get the most out of every day. I am a man in a hurry. And one of the first things I realized is that if I train my body to sleep for five hours a day, I can get more hours to chase my dreams. Then I realized that having more time is only half the battle won. So the second thing I do is manage my energy level. I stay fit through the three hours of golf and the one hour I spend every evening in the gym. Nasha makes sure that for each meeting I have a one-line summary of the expected outcome before I start. I spend the first five minutes of every meeting trying to agree on what both sides expect to achieve by the end of it. The last five minutes are to summarize the action items and next steps. Try it out.' BS's gold watch glittered with each gesture of his hand.

Rohan, Nasha and Kabir were fun to work with. We all lived on different floors of the same multistoreyed building in Connaught Place, barely five minutes from the office. Yet we never saw each other in the apartment complex. It was as if our relationship ended at the office and this was a different world.

Balwan Singh had a permanent reservation at the Grande Suite of the Taj. When we saw the black BMW drive away (with Nasha in the back seat with BS), we would breathe a collective sigh of relief. Rohan would pull out his Marlboro cigarettes and Kabir would order dinner for the three of us. We would occasionally help ourselves to a bottle of chilled beer from BS's pantry supplies. One such evening, we laughed together about how we all worked twelve hours a day on the adrenalin rush that the job provided.

'I wonder where BS gets his energy from,' I said. I was dropping with exhaustion.

Rohan spoke around the Marlboro dangling from the corner of his lips. 'From the exercises he does with Nasha. She is hot, man.'

Kabir reminded us, 'Don't even think about her unless you want death by castration.'

He sprang up and ran to answer the phone that was ringing with a sense of urgency. He gestured to us to leave the room. We ignored the sign language and shamelessly eavesdropped.

Rohan winked at me and said, 'That has to be Kabir's girlfriend Lilette. She has a knack for knowing when BS has left the office. Just watch the bastard coochie-coo into the phone. Lucky dog. She is a nice girl.'

Kabir was trying to be very discreet as he whispered, 'So do I... very much... of course... sure... on Sunday. Talk to you later. Bye.'

'Was that Lilette?' I asked.

'How did you guess?' Kabir enquired.

'You don't need to be a genius to figure out what the other person was saying. So it had to be Lilette.' Rohan stubbed out his cigarette.

'Do you have a girlfriend, Abbey?' This was the first time someone had asked me the question since Ayesha left.

'Actually, I am kind of... well no, not really...' I stammered.

'We'll find out, you bastard. We have our methods of interrogation,' Kabir threatened me.

I changed the topic and said, 'Since BS is going on vacation for two weeks, I am planning to really enjoy the coming weekend and get my apartment in order. I just don't get time to do anything after I leave the office. Though, to be fair, BS did warn me about the crazy pace.'

Rohan and Kabir had started working in the Chairman's office a year before I had. They seemed to know it all while I was still fumbling around, finding my way in this new world. There were days when I missed Captain Sobti's advice and guidance. Things were so different here, far from the dirt and soot of the field. We were thinking of larger challenges for the corporation rather than spending our day doing mundane stuff like sanctioning loans to workers or visiting them at home. Meeting Sohanlal Negi and his cronies was the most important task I had had in the factory. Being in the Chairman's office seemed more appropriate training for what I hoped would be my next big role. Most of the projects required me to work with the big man himself, and I felt I was learning a lot.

Most of all, I noticed how everyone seemed to treat me differently just because I was now a part of the

Chairman's office. So a phone call to the Balwanpur factory would get me instant results. Compliance was taken for granted. I was beginning to love this newfound authority to make things happen. If anything took a tad longer than I thought necessary, I would drop the magic initials of the Chairman and everything would fall into place. I used this clout to initiate a couple of projects: a hospital in Balwanpur with a special unit to treat patients with severe burn injuries and a club where senior citizens of the township could socialize. I took Captain Sobti's advice and proposed that both projects be named after Balwan Singh's parents. That was a surefire way to get the money sanctioned.

Then there was Keya. Every weekend, if not every second day, we met for dinner.

Once when I was in MIJ and was sitting at Daadu's Dhaba with Keya, sipping the syrupy sweet tea, she had asked me what attracted me to a woman.

Without thinking, I had said, 'A hundred-watt smile like yours, Keya. That's what sparks off the chemistry. A smile from a stranger is the most irresistible invite I can think of.'

Keya came over on Sunday morning, wearing a light pink cotton kurta and jeans. She pointed to her tiny silver earrings to indicate to me that they were new and that I should not forget to notice them. She was wearing a lovely pair of kolhapuri slippers and the silver ring on her toe gleamed. She gave me a hug and announced that she had just learnt a new recipe that she had to try out right away.

'Wow, I didn't know you were fond of cooking. Look, my kitchen here is rather limited. I rarely cook at home. We'll have to go and buy the ingredients,' I said.

'I've got the ingredients. Now close your eyes,' she said, pulling out a small multicoloured oval-shaped can. She opened the lid and held it under my nose.

'It smells like tea leaves. What is it?' I said with my eyes shut.

'It smells like tea leaves because that's what it is. Abbey, do you know most human beings on this planet die without learning how to make tea? I once learnt meditation from a Buddhist monk. He was from a monastery in Ghoom, close to Darjeeling.'

'In Bengali, Ghoom means sleep,' I said, inhaling the fragrance of the tea leaves.

'May I Ghoom with you?' Keya asked.

It was one of those magical days. Vivaldi's *Four Seasons* played in the background as we cooked, or rather, as Keya cooked and I ate. A piece of four violin concertos written in 1723 seemed to take us through the shifting seasons of our own past as spring changed to summer and then to autumn and winter. I ran my fingers through her hair and Keya shuddered in response as the summer came to an end with the fury of a thunderstorm.

# FOURTEEN

Over the next two years, life in the Chairman's office was a happy blur. There was work, work and more work. Soon, the pattern became predictable, and that's always a dangerous sign for me. I knew by now that whenever I got a total grip over the work and put every piece of it in order, the job ceased to give me an adrenalin rush. I was beginning to feel the same now. Over the past two years I had managed to find ways to categorize and compartmentalize my work. I had learnt to anticipate the questions that BS would ask and I knew how to provide the information he needed before he asked for it.

Like every year, this year too, when Durga Puja came around, I spent time with Baba and Ma. As usual, they bought new clothes for me to wear for each of the four days. I protested to Ma that I wasn't a five-year-old any more, but you know how difficult it is to win an argument with your mother.

Ma wore an off-white silk saree with a red border when we visited one of the four puja venues at Chittaranjan Park – CR Park to Delhiites. This part of Delhi had everything that Calcutta had to offer, from colourful pandals to authentic Bong cuisine. Every puja day, Ma would get Baba, Asmita and me to fast until we had offered our morning prayers. That year, Asmita and I had a heated debate about my smoking before prayers.

'The idea is to not eat or drink before one has finished prayers. Smoking doesn't fall into either category. So what's the problem?' I asked Asmita, who was looking rather pretty in a saree that she had draped by herself for the first time.

'It's pointless arguing with you. Let me go and ask Ma what she thinks of this…' Asmita threatened.

'Oh, all right.' I put away my cigarettes.

'And you have to promise never to call me Ass ever again. Or you have to pay a fine of five hundred rupees each time you make the mistake.'

'At that rate I will be able to call you Ass barely ten times a month. That's not adequate,' I reasoned.

Getting licences for the factory from the ministries took forever under the licence-raj. So BS spent the better part of the week micro-managing our efforts. Every Friday, he would head home to Balwanpur, only to be back by Monday afternoon, to put us under the microscope again.Whenever BS travelled out of Delhi, either to Balwanpur or to some other city, it was downtime for the team. Attendance in the office was restricted strictly to the office hours. We would all catch up with our pending work. That was also the time when we got to actually enjoy a five-day week. Also, every year BS went on vacation to some exotic location or the other, from 20 December until 10 January. Those dates were fixed. It was equally well-known that he would go for a short vacation to Switzerland between 1 and 10 July. This was one aspect of his life that remained unchanged, perhaps to compensate for the enormous unpredictability of everything else. I think Captain Sobti's law of paradoxes explained it well.

He had once told me over a glass of Mai Tai and a cigar, 'Remember, Abbey, the law of paradoxes works everywhere. Spend like a pauper to splurge like a king. If you are careful with your money in your youth, you will be able to live well in your old age. If you live like an old man when you are young, you will live like a young man in your old age. The day you join your first job is when you need to start planning for your retirement. Unfortunately, that time seems so far away that we wait until we've actually retired. At best, some people plan for it five years ahead, but by then it is too late.'

'So Captain, to apply this law of paradoxes, if we want to make changes rapidly in the company, we should go slow initially. Am I right?'

'Yes. I wish you could be in the factory with me at this time of transition. You need to be the new face of the management, Abbey. And Arai is the leader the company needs. He will never trust me because he sees Negi as being aligned very closely to me. He trusts you purely because of that snakes-to-riches scheme that you launched.'

'Failure in the factory will make you succeed in the head office, according to the law of paradoxes! Don't remind me of that scheme, Captain. It was such a dumb move. I still feel embarrassed when I think of it.'

'Those who have failed are also the likeliest to succeed. Beware of anyone who tells you that he or she has never failed. Arai sees you as a person with a heart. As someone who cares about them. The factory needs you now, Abbey. There are major changes in the air. The next five years will redefine the way the company does business. I am getting tired now. So take over from me.' He got up from his armchair and yawned. 'I need to go to bed now. I have a call with the Minister of Industries tomorrow. And it may well be the beginning of a change in Balwanpur Industries,' he said mysteriously before walking away in a haze of cigar smoke.

I didn't take up the invitation. It was not my cherished desire to leave Delhi and the glamour of the corporate office and move to Balwanpur. The place never failed to remind me of Ayesha and my failed marriage.

One day, not long after, Kabir, Rohan and I decided to go out for lunch. BS was away on one of his foreign jaunts and we were enjoying the relaxed pace of work. But strange as it might sound, we were all suffering from withdrawal symptoms. Kabir had invited his girlfriend Lilette to meet him somewhere for coffee. So after lunch he decided to abandon us. I decided to stop and buy some cigarettes from the paanwallah at the corner of Regal cinema. As I counted out change, someone tapped me on the shoulder. It was Priya. This was the first time I was meeting her after that last disastrous encounter. She had not come for my wedding, nor had Kapil.

'You have completely disappeared from the face of this earth, Abbey. Where have you been? How is Ayesha? Do you have a photo? I missed the wedding. It must have been a lot of fun.' Priya was her usual self.

There was no hint of bitterness in her voice.

'Priya, meet my colleague Rohan. How have you been? Are you still singing?' I asked, my tone slightly formal, and avoiding the question about Ayesha altogether. I knew Rohan would grill me later.

'Kapil wanted to set up a studio. He said it would give him the opportunity to do something different from accounting. I manage the studio on his behalf. You should come and see it sometime, Abbey. It's called Jingle Belles. Do you like the name? I love it. I chose it because ours is the only sound studio in Delhi which is managed entirely by women. A friend of mine, Tara, is the sound engineer. She has just graduated from the Film Institute at Pune. She is amazing. I get to do a few jingles myself. In fact, we just released a cassette of old Hindi film songs for children. Let me see if I have a copy.' Priya started to rummage through her Gurjari bag.

'You have to sign it for me, Priya. I don't have a single cassette that's been signed by the singer.' I was impressed with her determination to chase her dreams.

'I have only one cassette left. Rohan, I'll send one to you next week. I am off to Bombay this evening to promote the album. Wish you could come for the launch. Kapil has some very powerful clients from Bollywood. He files their tax returns. You know that always helps! They are all endorsing my music. Show me your wife's photo, Abbey. She must be really pretty for you to have fallen for her. You must forgive me for not coming to the wedding bash. I was hospitalized that week – nothing major, just food poisoning.'

'Actually, Ayesha is in the US. I don't have a picture right now, but I'll remember to show you the wedding snaps.' I leaned over to hug her. 'I need to go back to the office. See you soon, Priya. Say hi to Kapil for me.'

'Abbey, just one thing. Kapil and I got married last year.' Priya walked off without making eye contact with me.

I was caught off-guard.

*So Kapil, the valiant one, had stepped in to save the damsel in distress.*

*Stop finding fault, Abbey. Kapil doesn't just have a heart, he also has guts – unlike some others we know.*

*I agree it was nice of him to marry Priya.*

*Thanks, Abbey. Your approval is really important.*

I needed to get back to the office. There was a project I was working on that needed my attention. Rohan had not probed and I did not offer to explain. The English language has two different words to describe a colleague and a friend, Captain had said. Since then my personal life had become out of bounds for my colleagues.

My relationship with Keya, meanwhile, settled into

دوست،

This means DOST
or The Friend

In the Sufi tradition
the Master is called The Friend.
So beautiful --- Wonder if
I will ever meet
a wandering dervish?

love Urdu
wish I knew
how to write
and read. Urdu was made
for poetry, thirst,
passion, love...
fanaah, love...
English is for
accountants.

where to go
What to do
What makes
me happy??

my graphic nataraja

Too many thoughts
Make your mind a
spagetti.

Every one tells
me I am too intense
Am I?

Reminds me ~
must pick up
some pesto and
olives.

हर शादी
रिश्ता नहीं होता
हर रिश्ता
शादी नहीं

I want
to die of
love not
boredom.

'So that I can be close to you. The other option would have been to work with the paanwallah near Regal. I could meet you everyday when you stopped to buy cigarettes.' She laughed and kissed my palm.

Just when I thought I had discovered a pattern in her behaviour, Keya would find something new to espouse and I would have to start afresh. She always lived in the present. Neither the past nor the future had any particular significance for her.

One night she woke me up at 2 a.m. with a phone call to announce that I had missed something really important. I instantly thought of deadlines at work. After a two-minute silence she told me that it had been raining for the past fifteen minutes and that I should instantly go for a walk in the rain. I wanted to put the phone down and go to sleep. But knowing Keya, that would have meant the end of our relationship. So I stayed up and heard her describe the raindrops as they fell on her window and dripped along the glass pane.

She spent most weekends at my apartment. Often, she would hide a note with a few lines from a poem or a ghazal scribbled on it. I would stumble upon these love notes at odd times and in the strangest of places. Under the pillow, stuck on the bathroom mirror, taped to a bottle of wine. I was convinced that she had memorized every love poem ever written on the planet. Keya barely slept for four or five hours at night. Life is too short to miss a single sunrise or sunset, she said.

One evening in July, I got caught in an unexpected

shower. I was just changing into dry clothes when I heard an urgent knock on the door. It was Keya. She ran into the apartment, grabbed some clothes and threw them into her favourite backpack. Then she ran out. I feared the worst.

*What could have possibly happened? Maybe someone has been hospitalized.*

I followed her into the waiting taxi. She just looked out of the window silently. I knew she wanted to be left alone, so I held her hand and did not speak, either. The cab's headlights were on and it was making its way towards the highway.

'Where are we going?' I asked no one in particular.

'To Agra, sir,' said the driver of the cab.

'To see the Taj Mahal by moonlight. Only four hundred people are allowed to visit the Taj on a full moon night. I have a lunar calendar in my office, Abbey. I had completely forgotten that tonight is a full moon night. Aren't you glad I remembered? It rained in the evening and I knew that meant I had forgotten something.'

'I have to send a folder to Balwan Singh tomorrow morning. I'll get sacked if I don't. Keya, are you crazy? Let's go back... please? We'll go next month and I promise you it will rain that night. I need to give that folder to...'

'I don't think it will rain that night. This is a once in a lifetime opportunity, Abbey. If Balwan Singh gets upset with you, please tell him what Sahir Ludhianvi said...'

'Don't be childish, Keya. I need to get that folder to BS. He needs it for a meeting and he doesn't care a hoot about what Sahir Ludhianvi has to say. Balwan Singh will go completely ballistic if I miss the deadline. By the way, if it rains, how will you see the Taj by the moonlight? Okay, relax! We ARE on our way to the Taj. So stop sulking.' I knew I couldn't fight the tears in Keya's eyes.

So we drove all the way to the Taj and saw it by moonlight. It was a truly magical experience. The last time I saw it, I was ten years old. All I remembered was that the marble was burning hot and I tried walking like a penguin to minimize contact with the white stone. This was different. The marble was cool and freshly washed by the rain. And what had seemed like carvings at the entrance to the Taj turned out to be verses from the Koran. We sat on a marble bench in the garden, facing the Taj, and stared at it.

'The sky had promised me that it would rain tonight. Whenever the thought flashes in her mind you see the flash of lightning,' Keya murmured.

From the Taj, we drove for an hour to reach Fatehpur Sikri, the tomb of Shaykh Salim Chishti. The Mughal emperor Akbar had prayed to Salim Chishti for a male heir to the throne. And he had got one.

'Why the hell are we going there? We need to pray that we do NOT have any,' I told Keya as soon as she told me about the legend.

'Abbey, you should see the tomb of Salim Chishti. The filigree work in marble is amazing. You and I will make a wish by tying a piece of thread to the marble screen of the tomb. I believe you have to come back to untie the knot once your wish has been fulfilled.'

'That's silly. Look at the number of people who have asked the saint for something or the other. There are thousands of threads tied to every square inch of the screen. How would I even identify the knot that we tied?' I asked Keya when we finally stood by the majestic tomb.

'That's easy, Abbey. When you come here and undo a knot, that's when the saint fulfils the wish of the person who actually tied that thread. My wish will be granted when some stranger unties the knot that I am tying tonight,' she said as she looked at me and closed her eyes to make a wish. 'I want to make it easy for someone to undo this knot.'

## FIFTEEN

Let me just say that I did not get that folder to Balwan Singh in time for his meeting. BS was livid. He started giving me cold vibes. I thought that was crazy. Over the past two years, ever since I'd moved into this new assignment, I'd bust my guts trying to put together good ideas for him. Why should a solitary goof-up qualify me for corporate Siberia?

I shared my angst with Rohan and Kabir. They suggested that I speak to Nasha and take her help in trying to patch things up with BS. She was quite sympathetic to my cause. She suggested that I try to do an innovative write-up on stuff we could do in HR and share it with BS. So Rohan, Kabir, Nasha and I sat down to brainstorm.

'Let's meet this evening at your apartment and get drunk. We're sure to come up with some offbeat ideas,' Rohan suggested.

'Let's look at ideas that are truly cutting edge.' Kabir was already thumbing through a book by Charles Clark called *Brainstorming: How to Create Successful Ideas.*

I tried to recall what Rascal Rusty had said about brainstorming techniques. Basically, you could take any idea and add/subtract/multiply/divide it to find a new thought. He had given me a pencil and told me to start listing as many ways of using a pencil as I could think of.

'Writing is one usage. In that sense, writing a song and writing a story, both refer to the same usage. But if you say you can use a pencil to create a game, that's a new usage,' Rusty had said.

I had been surprised that after five minutes of effort we were able to come up with sixty-two new ideas on how to use a pencil. It occurred to me that I should ask Rusty for help now. He would come up with a new perspective. So I looked up his details in my diary and dialled his number in Dubai. He took a moment to place me.

'It's not as if you call every day, you crazy fucker. You are calling me after five years. How is work?' said Rusty in a voice that betrayed a slight hint of an accent that I was not familiar with.

'Rusty, I need help desperately to present a really unique idea on HR to my Chairman. Is there something you can suggest? Have you come across anything new and interesting?'

'Hmm, let me see. Maybe you should question the basics of HR policy, Abbey. I've been thinking about this on and off, never quite formulated it. Have you ever wondered why people earn the least when they need money the most? When you start working, you want to buy a house, a car, you want to travel abroad and yet, that's when you earn the least. Then, towards the end of your career, you earn the most – at a time when you can't enjoy the goodies. You have an expense account when the doctor advises you to watch your cholesterol and sugar and what have you. Life is so fucking unfair.

'Maybe what you should recommend is that you get an actuary to estimate how much a person is likely to earn at the end of his lifetime. Then pay him that salary and each year decrease the amount he would have earned by way of increment. The young kids will be happy because they wouldn't otherwise see that kind of money. The older folk would have no issues because they would have already provided for everything while they were young. I need to go now, Abbey. Take a trip to Dubai. I'll show you what the good life is all about.' The phone went dead.

I shared the idea with Rohan, Kabir and Nasha. They loved it. We spent the entire night working to put together a compelling case for this revolutionary concept. Rohan and Kabir worked out the financial impact of the decision and how we could phase in the concept in practice. We were very excited about presenting it the next morning.

I went back to my apartment and changed into my best blue shirt and steel grey trousers. I combed my hair and admired myself in the mirror for a fleeting second before I walked over to the office, ready to rock the world.

BS wasn't in the best of moods. At least, he didn't seem very open to a revolutionary thought process in HR. He was not ready to let Balwanpur Industries appear on the cover of *Fortune* magazine as an example of how an Indian company had redefined the system. Maybe he was a person who found it difficult to forgive. Whatever the reason, he totally rejected my grand idea. I was depressed. Then again, it was Rascal Rusty's idea that I had built upon. So maybe the rejection slip had gone to Rusty, I consoled myself.

I called up Rusty and told him that his idea had been rejected and that I was still a prime candidate for transportation to the boondocks – in this case, the Balwanpur factory. Rascal Rusty was not even remotely apologetic for having nearly destroyed my career.

He said, 'Does he have a trend monitoring cell in the corporate office?'

I shook my head to indicate that he didn't and then realized I had to say it aloud so Rusty could hear.

'The most important survival strategy for a company is to have people in their organization who can read societal trends. These trends will give the company a sneak preview of the way the consumers are going to change. From what I can see, India is ready to join the consumerist societies of the west. It is, after all, a land of entrepreneurs. If the government could do something to unleash that force and channelize it, we could be the next big thing. What trends have you observed of late? By that I mean societal or corporate trends and not fashion trends, bastard!' Rusty added, just in time to prevent me from embarrassing myself.

'I notice that salaries in India are rising. That's a recent trend. Some companies are paying eight to ten times the salary for the same job that I am doing at Balwanpur. All the multinational corporations are paying the earth to their employees. Maybe I should change jobs too, and work for an MNC. It certainly sounds much more glamorous.'

'In short, you are saying that you would rather work for a gora boss? What makes you think that he would be better than a desi boss? Yours is the typical mentality of someone whose ancestors were ruled by the angrez for two hundred years. There are good managers and bad managers. It has nothing to do with nationality or skin colour,' Rusty chided me.

'Okay, so tell me how to look for trends. I want to be one of those trend watchers.' I was tickled by the idea.

'Go through the magazines of the last six months. Look for human interest stories in the popular press. Tell me what themes and topics seem to be coming up repeatedly.'

'Off the cuff, I can tell you that there are lots of stories about globalization – is it a boon or a curse? There are stories about the westernization of Indian society and how traditional values are getting diluted. Last week, three magazines carried stories about the rising rate of divorce in India. So what trends do you see in these stories?' I asked.

'They all point to the fact that corporate India will lead the social transformation. A globalized workplace will mean increasing exposure to the west. That in turn will make it easy for people to introduce western concepts of living in our society. So Abbey, expect to see a greater craze for western clothes, fashion, movies, and yet a desire among the youth to hold on to purist traditions. A paradox of sorts...'

'Exactly! The law of paradoxes would say that the more western we are, the stronger our faith in tradition. We should probably expect to see more women in the workplace. Hey, that would be good.' I liked what I imagined the workplace of the future to be.

'Right now, you HR people have no idea how to make offices women friendly. Other than providing for a ladies' washroom and maternity benefits, companies don't have any policies that are designed to get more women into the workplace. So here is what you should suggest to your Chairman. Start a campaign to get more women in. Be a frontrunner in this area.'

'You always come up with clever stuff, bugger. But it sounds fairly radical. I don't think Balwan Singh will agree to something so drastic. He is a very traditional sort of guy – except when it comes to his own sex life. He has this hot chick called Nasha in the office...' I started to tell Rusty, when he interrupted me.

'HR professionals need to work closely with the people in marketing. Maybe that's another prediction for the future. Every company spends so much on consumer research, yet we have never heard of a company that does employee research. Isn't that strange? So many of the HR folk are still recycling stupid statements like "People are our most important assets." Whenever I see that line, I want to scratch out the "t" in "assets".' Rusty started to laugh hysterically.

Then he broke off abruptly and asked, 'By the way, what happened between Ayesha and you? I bumped into her at the Waldorf Astoria when I was in New York last month. She now runs a small boutique called Mystical Dreams in Manhattan. I think it was on Fifth Avenue. She must have a rich financier to be able to afford that address. She told me that you guys were living apart. I had heard rumours, of course, but what's the truth, Abbey?'

I found myself thinking of Captain Sobti as I said calmly, 'Ayesha and I are such different people. We felt it was better to move on rather than stay together and suffer. We were making each other miserable. She is probably much happier now than she was with me.'

'I don't know about that. She did seem to miss you, Abbey. She was telling me that living in the Big Apple tends to get very mechanical and hectic.'

'She preferred to be a part of New York rather than spend her life shuttling between Delhi and Balwanpur. I think she did the right thing. Life is too short. Ayesha has had the courage to be her own self, to chase her dreams. And I think that is admirable. Mark my words, Rusty, she will be the first girl in our batch to appear on the cover of *Fortune* magazine.' I found myself defending Ayesha.

Rusty didn't take the bait, and we hung up after exchanging some more pleasantries.

In the days that followed, Balwan Singh appeared to be

preoccupied. Sobti was in town and he and Balwan Singh spent days together, poring over balance sheets and the profit and loss accounts that Kabir had to prepare, the sales and marketing plans for the next three years that Rohan put together a million versions of, and numerous calculations of employee costs that I had to produce at a moment's notice. Even the usually well-organized Nasha seemed distant and stressed. Rohan, Kabir, Nasha and I spent all our waking hours in the office.

One evening, I called up Mrs Dayal at the factory. She would know what was going on, if anybody did. What she told me shocked me beyond belief.

'Balwanpur Industries is up for sale. They say that Balwan Singhji has already found a buyer and he is just waiting for the right price. Kamal Kant Shah of the K.K. Shah Group of Industries is reportedly the buyer.'

What could this mean? Would the new owner sack all the old employees and bring in his team of managers? It suddenly occurred to me that I might soon be without a job.

I was confused. Should I share my newfound knowledge with the other three? Maybe among the four of us we could piece together some information that would throw more light on the scenario. But prudence got the better of me.

*What if they sneak to BS that I'm spreading rumours?*

*They are your friends. Why would they do something like that?*

*Sobti had said that the English language distinguishes between friends and colleagues.*

*Maybe you should revise that – friends can be colleagues, but colleagues cannot be friends.*

*Maybe you should do some research on the group, instead of wallowing in self-pity.*

Winter was setting in. I looked at the calendar. It was Monday, 11 December 1989. That meant nine days of work before BS took his winter vacation. Apparently, he was off to the US. I wondered if Nasha was going with him. Not that it was any of my business – which was precisely why it took up so much mind space!

I tried to ask a few people about the K.K. Shah Group (KKSGI, we had called it at MIJ, pronounced Cakes-GI). But all my MIJ mates could tell me was that Gopher had joined the group a year ago. My question aroused considerable curiosity: Why did I want to know about the group? Was I contemplating joining them? Did I have an offer already? Gosh, what an inquisitive bunch!

I tried reading up. The *Business Magnate* had done a cover story on the group three months ago. I had casually glanced through the piece then, but not much had registered. I tried to look up Balwan Singh's files of paper cuttings. They contained material on companies ranging from Apollo Tyres to Zenith Computers, but the KKSGI set of clippings was missing. The magazines were arranged chronologically in the library in BS's office. Only the issue of the *Business Magnate* with the KKSGI story was not in its place. Clearly, I would have to do some research on my own, and discreetly.

On Friday evening, Nasha, Rohan and Kabir decided

we should watch a movie. I said I had a headache and needed to be alone. I walked with them to the main door to make sure they left. That was when the two folders on the corner table caught my attention. The missing issue of the *Business Magnate* and the bunch of paper clippings on the K.K. Shah Group were lying there, out where anybody could read them. Here was my chance.

After I read through it all, I made copious notes. I had just put away everything when the door opened and I saw Nasha, Kabir and Rohan grinning at me.

'Abbey, you lied to us about having a headache. You could have just told us you wanted to research the group. We would have given you the papers,' said Rohan.

'So you guys have all been in on this. Why didn't you tell me?' I challenged the three of them, especially Nasha, who was laughing hysterically.

'Each of us has been working on some aspect of the possible sale. The Shah group thinks that Balwanpur's goodwill and market share make it an attractive jewel to have in their kitty,' said Kabir, who was the finance whiz kid on our team. 'The technical term for it is Mergers and Acquisitions, or M&A as the business media calls it.'

I went back home and lay flat on my back, thinking about what the M&A would mean for Balwanpur Industries.

The thought of being in the same company as Gopher was acutely unpleasant. I wondered whether he would be senior to me, or at the same level in the hierarchy. Given that he had joined them a year earlier, there was every chance that he would be a rung ahead. I hoped like hell that I would not be in the same department as he was. Maybe he had switched to marketing or something. I thought of all the times I had been nasty and sarcastic while dealing with him. Surely he would not be vindictive because of that. Then again, this was Gopher, I reminded myself. He could set the gold standard for being an asshole.

## Sixteen

Gur and Neetika called to invite me over for dinner on my birthday. They were also trying to reach other batchmates of ours from MIJ. I had, until now, managed to wriggle out of every invitation to MIJ gatherings. It was silly, but I just didn't feel comfortable being with them. I knew the conversation would inevitably veer towards Ayesha and our break-up – or the lack of it. But Gur and Neats were insistent. We had bumped into each other one afternoon, while I was buying cigarettes from my paanwallah at Regal. I felt cornered. Not only did I work in the heart of CP, I even lived there. And every human being on the planet seemed to land up in CP to watch a film or eat out, or visit the underground shopping complex at Palika Bazar.

I groped for a way out. Since 16 November happened to be a Thursday, I told them I would probably be working late anyway, so we should keep the celebration for the following Saturday, instead. That would give me time to find a new reason to ditch them, I figured. Neetika said birthdays should be celebrated on the actual day or else it didn't feel like a birthday celebration. Gur instantly agreed and said it would be like celebrating New Year's on 2 January. I suggested that we call it, not a birthday celebration, but an LTNB – Long Time No Booze party. But they chipped away at all my protests and excuses one by one.

On the day itself, Baba, Ma and Asmita were the first to call and wish me. Keya had slipped away in the morning as usual, but a small gift-wrapped box sat on my bedside table, along with a birthday card. The box was empty. The card simply stated:

To my adorable Scorpio,

The moments that we spent together are real and yet you cannot see them. The next time we spend time together, can we lock away one such moment? Happy Birthday, Abbey.

Love,

K

After work, I went straight to the beautiful house in Defence Colony that Gur and Neetika rented. Neats had done it up so beautifully that I could not help comment on how she had managed to civilize Gur. He had been assigned the task of watering (what seemed to look like) the entire rain forest in their garden. There was a lovely bar set up in the veranda, Gur informed me. We opened a bottle of beer each and chatted idly about our batchmates. Gur and Neetika seemed to be in touch with everyone at MIJ.

Gur said, 'Joy has just got a promotion and become Personnel Manager. Can you believe that? He has a team of ten people reporting to him. Pappu has started his own business. In his first job, he had the keys to their branch office in South Extension. Every Monday he would oversleep and his office staff had to wait outside until he landed up. One day he decided to spare everyone the agony and started his own business of selling electrical motors.'

Gur reached for a second beer. 'You know Abbey, we invited Arunesh to our wedding anniversary party. He has bought himself a brand new Fender guitar and has teamed up with a rock band called Beat Routes. Now he is planning to quit his job and become a guitarist with the band. He has composed ten songs and has recorded them at a studio run entirely by women. Isn't that crazy?'

'What is so crazy about women running a studio?' Neats got up to get us something to eat.

'No, I meant the idea of Arunesh quitting his job to become a rock guitarist.'

'I know about the studio, it's called Jingle Belles,' I said, feeling happy for Priya.

Neats handed us a plate of sizzling hot kababs. She said, 'Vishy has done the craziest thing possible. He has formed a religious sect and become a spiritual leader. He has grown his hair and beard and lives in an ashram in some remote part of Tamil Nadu. I went to my sister-in-law's house the other day and met her neighbour Mrs Srinivasan, who is a staunch devotee of Swami Vishwanand. She tried to sell me some tapes of his discourses. When I saw the photo on the cover I realized it was our own Vishy – complete with a beard and long hair. I have a copy of the tape. He runs a ten-day meditation camp that a lot of corporate houses are sending people to. I believe Rusty gave him the idea.'

'That's interesting. What's the latest with you guys? Neats, is Gur treating you well? Is he behaving himself? I can see he has put on at least ten kilos, and so have you,' I added.

'We should tell you the good news. Neats is becoming a mother,' said Gur, embarrassed and proud at the same time.

'Congrats! Who is the father?' I asked.

He chucked a salted peanut at me. 'We need to keep the kid away from evil influences. Neats, keep the kiddo away from Abbey.'

'Have you chosen a civilized name for the kid or will you opt for a unisex Punjabi name like Ranjeet Singh if it is a boy and Ranjeet Kaur if it is a girl? Takes the suspense out of it,' I joked.

Gur and Neats seemed so happy together. They showed me pictures of their recent trip to Europe. Neats showed me all the clothes they had bought and told me how their suitcases had got left behind in Amsterdam. Gur told me about the 'topless bars' of Europe. I was planning a research paper on the subject myself, I told them.

Neats pulled out some Swiss chocolates and gave me five huge bars to take home with me. My birthday present, she said.

They had bought a fantastic music system from

Germany. We played all the Deep Purple, Queen and Dylan numbers that we used to listen to at MIJ. It was close to midnight when they dropped me back to my apartment. I told them I would take a cab back, but they insisted that they enjoyed the drive to CP and back. A million times the next day, I found myself feeling just a tad jealous as I compared their marriage to mine. Would it have been different if I had married Keya instead?

The paanwallah at Regal was also where I met Divya Samtani, the snooty little thing from Railway Colony who had graduated from MIJ as part of the batch of '87. She was now working at the famous Global Village Bank as part of their marketing team. She had lost weight and looked different in her business suit. She told me as she handed me her business card that she was already Vice President, Marketing and was in town for the next two days in connection with a 'film shoot'.

'Divvy, you are making movies? Wow… surely you can find me a small role as a side-kick to the hero,' I said, excited all at once.

'Oh Abbey, stop making fun of me. I am shooting the latest commercial for the Global Village Bank. Haven't you seen my campaign "Give your heart to the bank with a heart"? It's all over television. Do you know, I even received an award from the Ad Council of India last month. I believe they are sending the commercial as our entry to several international advertising competitions.' At this point, Divya introduced me to the two assistants who were patiently waiting for us to finish our conversation.

'That's a radical thought for a bank commercial, isn't it? You could continue with that tagline forever. Just take the different parts of the body. Your next campaign should be "Give your ass to the bank..."' I was trying to be funny, but Divvy did not find it humorous at all.

'You have no business making fun of my campaign. You've always been jealous of my success. I am already a vice president at the bank, even though I am three batches junior to you. That's what bugs you, I know, but there's no need to be cheap. I am in a hurry. Bye.' Divvy walked off in a huff.

'Hey Divvy, I was just joking. It's a cool campaign, man,' I shouted after her, but all it got me was stares from passersby.

I paid for my cigarettes and walked back, trying to battle the voice in my head.

*It is true that you are still called Deputy Manager, HR while she is already Vice President.*

*Every company has a different system of designating its employees. In the Global Village Bank, even newborns are designated Vice President, Diapers or something like that.*

*Don't you want to be called Vice President, HR? Divya is obviously more successful than you. Accept that.*

*I am not competing with anyone.*

*Even Ayesha was called Manager, Personnel and that was three years ago. Five years after MIJ, you are still called Deputy Manager.*

I thought I should bring up the matter with Balwan Singh. If, after an MBA and five years of work, I was still not good enough to be called Manager, it was a waste of time for me to continue. But I would have to wait for BS to return from his vacation in the first week of January before I could talk to him.

I called up Keya and told her how worried I was that I would never be termed successful in my career. That everyone in my batch and ten batches junior to me was probably ahead of me anyway. I declared myself to be a total failure in life. Keya was plainly taken aback at how important the promotion and change of designation were to me. My life seemed to revolve around it. She told me that at the end of the day, all it meant was that the corporate sector seemed to be run by the print industry that churned out business cards.

'Isn't it silly, Keya, how you can give someone a new business card and get the right to kick him around for some more time,' I said philosophically as I let her draw stars on my elbow with her pen.

'The whole corporate sector runs on people's insecurities. What's worse, these are educated people who would try every unscrupulous act in the book to get ahead of their colleagues – all for the sake of a business card! Most people aspire to be a manager in one year and then aspire to be the manager's manager in the next and the manager's manager's manager thereafter. Is that all there is to life? I've told my office that if they ever promote me, I'll quit.'

'After a promotion you would get more money, Keya. That's always handy.' I had sparked off a career counselling session with Keya with that one remark.

'Yes, and I would have to give up all my time in the bargain. When you were in MIJ, you had a cheap portable mono tape recorder, but you had all the time to listen to music and learn the lyrics of your favourite songs. Now you have a fancy music system at home and no time to listen to music. Is that what you want to earn and get a promotion for?'

Sometimes, Keya could be totally out of touch with reality.

It was New Year's Eve and I was still in office. Keya had invited me to join the party at the Taj. They had some Brazilian dancers whose pictures had been plastered across the front page of every newspaper. Baba and Ma had assumed that like every other year I would join the celebrations at the Railway Club. I had to make a choice, and I chose to spend the evening with Keya. I booked a room at the hotel itself so that I wouldn't have to find my way back to my apartment through the hordes of drunken drivers honking away to express their joy or angst, as the case might be.

Keya and I had a blast dancing with the Brazilian babes (along with the two hundred other guests, I might add). At the stroke of midnight, as the countdown started, we held each other and kissed. She whispered, 'I love you,' and I echoed her words.

'Whatever you do at the stroke of midnight is what you will continue to do the most during the rest of the year.' Keya had her own theories on life.

'That's why most of the guys were hitting on the Brazilian babes at the stroke of midnight. Didn't you see that fat balding moron grab the lead dancer and smooch her at the stroke of midnight? That guy has a great year ahead of him for sure,' I said.

'I pity the girl. She'll be kissing fat, bald morons throughout the year,' Keya said with a sigh as we walked back to our room.

We spent the next morning at the coffee shop, tasting all the versions of coffee that they had, from different parts of the world. Keya and I ordered alternate flavours and kept going down the menu for the rest of the day. After having Colombian, Sumatran, Arabian and Kenyan coffee, I felt I needed to have some old-fashioned instant coffee – the kind that we used to get in MIJ at Daadu's Dhaba. Since Keya was obsessed with making the first day of the year as close to perfect as possible, we decided to go to Moti Mahal in Daryaganj for lunch and follow it up with dinner at Karim's. After dinner we came back to the hotel, where a pianist was playing songs on request.

Keya went up and asked him to play the theme from *Godfather* – 'Speak softly love'. We held hands as he played one enchanting melody after the other. At one point, Keya leaned over and told me that she would name her first-born Melody.

# Seventeen

Even after Balwan Singh returned, I couldn't bring myself to have that conversation about a promotion. It would have made me look desperate – which is exactly what I was, of course.

But one day, when BS seemed to be in a happy mood and I actually saw him practice an imaginary golf swing in the office, I knew I had to take my chance. I tentatively broached the subject. I told him that all my batchmates from MIJ were already earning way more than I was (of course, if you excluded Vishy, the average came down dramatically) and were all designated as manager or general manager or vice president. I hoped I would not have to present my business card to him to prove my case. I doubt if he knew what my designation was, or cared.

The result of my stumbling monologue was a five-minute silence when I could hear my heartbeat speed up. He just stood there staring at me.

After a while he said, 'Why don't you study the designations used in our company and standardize them all? I see some silly designations floating around. That

Ramadorai fellow in the factory is called Manager, Managers' Claims. Which idiot created that, I wonder. We should be in line with all the other companies. Why don't you study the subject and come back with a modern grade system and designations that will make everyone happy?'

What a clever move. I was now lumped with a huge problem. No matter what designation I proposed, some section or the other would be pissed off and I would be the poster boy for everyone to spit on. Shit!

I called Rascal Rusty and shared the problem with him.

Rusty thought for a minute and said, 'That's an easy one. Just upgrade everyone to a designation of the next level. The assistant manager gets redesignated as deputy manager. The deputy manager gets to be manager. The manager will be called senior manager and so on. The only one whose designation should not be changed is the chairman. He probably doesn't care about it anyway.'

I told him that what the Chairman wanted was a proper study of the grade system and a rationalization of the salary and benefits structure. This simplistic solution of redesignating the entire bunch was not going to help. Above all, the whole thing was simply meant to be an opportunity for me to get a better designation and some more money, it wasn't for me to rewrite the theory of evolution.

Rusty was unfazed. 'If you are going to create a grade system that will put all five hundred office staff into five grades from the existing thirty-eight, you can't win. Just imagine if you and your boss and his boss all went into the same category. You would love it while your bosses would kill you for making such a dumb move. On the other hand, if personnel executive, assistant manager and deputy manager were to be clubbed together as one category, you would be miserable because you would see it as a huge demotion.'

I trusted Rusty's foresight. I asked him, 'So what is the solution to this mess, Rusty? Don't create problems for me. I have enough enemies and don't need any more.'

'Give the job to a consultant,' said Rusty. 'They will take a year to do it and will charge one-tenth of the group's profits as their fee. They will create complicated charts and do regression analysis of a million variables. Anyone who questions their recommendations will be asked to sit through a presentation that will contain phrases like "multivariate analysis of market forces", which will ensure that nobody questions the recommendations. They may crib among themselves but they will never be able to win the argument with the consultant. You can just shrug your shoulder and say that the consultants' recommendations have been accepted wholeheartedly by the chairman and the other directors. That way, the rumblings will die down in a few months.'

'What if my designation is the one that gets downgraded? Then I will be worse off after this exercise.' I had some real fears about the outcome.

'Make sure the consultants know that you have the final authority to appoint them for the project and that you will be the one to sign the final bill. Your being in the Chairman's office will ensure that the consultants treat you with deference. They will make sure that they recommend your move to a much higher position, so they will continue to be hired by you in future.'

This seemed like a smart idea. I was really pleased with Rusty.

*You idiot! If the consultant takes one year to complete the project, you will have to wait until then for your new designation. You will be stuck with that lousy Deputy Manager, HR designation for yet another year.*

*Why is it that I am always the chosen one to remain in a state of suspended animation? My marriage to Ayesha is in that state. Now even my work life is in a state that can only be described as being Somewhat Pregnant!*

I sat up for the next few days and nights and put together a proposal for Balwan Singh's approval. I did some research on HR consultants who were known for doing this kind of work. In the end, I was quite pleased with the impressive looking document I had put together for His Majesty.

Balwan Singh flipped through the pages cursorily and yawned. I doubt if it was humanly possible to read a few words, leave alone a few pages of that impressive tome in the time he gave it.

'Good. This is a good proposal. Why don't we just give people the opportunity to write fancy designations on their business cards? Meanwhile, let the consultants tell us how to put this grade structure in place for our internal purposes. No one will know how they are classified by the personnel department,' said Balwan Singh, barely managing to conceal his boredom.

'The HR classification is also important. It determines the salary and perks that people get.' I was annoyed that BS still used the archaic term, personnel department.

'Abbey, suppose you could print your designation on your business card as Vice President, Personnel or maybe I should say Vice President, Human Resources. Wouldn't that be a good starting point? Next, you would want to change the external symbols of hierarchy, like the kind of house you live in and the make of the car in your garage. If we took care of these, what we pay would be of lesser consequence. Is that a fair statement?' Balwan Singh was clearly on to something.

'I think... we should... probably...' I was not sure what stance to adopt, not until I took Rusty's advice on the matter.

The following Monday, when I reached the office, I saw a set of visiting cards on my desk that said 'Vice President, Human Resources' in place of my old designation. I looked at the date on the calendar. It was Monday, 2 April 1990. So it couldn't be some jerk's idea of an April Fool's Day prank. I noticed Rohan and Kabir standing at the door watching my reaction.

'Come in, you dogs!' I invited them in, barely able to conceal my excitement.

'Congratulations, Mr Vice President, sir!' Kabir bowed low as he spoke.

'Thanks, but this is no big deal. I don't think anyone

here cares about salaries and designations and all that. We all work here because we enjoy the work. The recognition is incidental. I really don't think of myself as any better than you just because I am a vice president,' I started, not believing a single word that I said.

Rohan punctured my rapidly bloating ego by saying, 'Stop pontificating, you crazy bugger. Kabir and I have also become vice presidents. Everyone in the Chairman's office has been redesignated. Let's go out and get drunk this evening. Nasha has a fancy visiting card too. I forget what she is called now, but it's really cool.'

Rohan, Kabir, Nasha and I headed out to the Taj straight after work. I called to see if Keya was free to join us, but she was away on a sales call and was not expected to be back in office that day. So it was just the four of us who celebrated. It's amazing how much happiness a reprinted business card can bring. I was dying to flash it at Divya Samtani who had assumed that just because she was a vice president, the rest of the world could be looked down upon. Sadly, all evening, there there wasn't a single occasion for me to show off my new card.

I called home and told Baba about my promotion. I hesitated for a second before using the word 'promotion' but then decided to go ahead anyway. Ma immediately suggested that I go to a temple and thank God for his blessings. Baba told me that I should now become more responsible and work harder so that I could live up to the trust the company had placed in me. Asmita wanted me to take her out for dinner.

I realized that in the frenzy of the celebrations, I had not thanked the Chairman or Captain Sobti. Then I reasoned that Sobti may not have had anything to with this decision. I was sure I had earned it through sheer hard work. So I walked into the Chairman's office next morning, prepared to be effusive. Balwan Singh was sitting in his chair with a strange expression on his face, as though he was in pain. Before I could say anything, he collapsed. I wasn't quick enough to stop him from falling off the chair. He clutched his chest as he writhed on the floor. I rushed out to inform Nasha and then called the All India Institute of Medical Sciences for an ambulance.

Balwan Singh had suffered a massive cardiac arrest. The doctors at AIIMS complimented me on my prompt action that enabled them to save his life. His wife and daughter were informed. They came down from Balwanpur accompanied by the directors. His wife Mrs Mohini Singh held my hand and started to thank me for saving her husband's life. Halfway through, she broke down. Their daughter Nikita also came up to me to say thanks. Then it was the turn of the directors. I wondered if they were secretly disappointed that Balwan Singh had survived. It must be tempting to think of taking over from him. I looked at Balwan Singh lying there and, to my surprise, felt a strong urge to pray for his recovery. I had always seen him completely in charge of himself and everyone else. It felt wrong somehow to see him lying unconscious with tubes and needles stuck all over his body.

I prayed for his recovery. I rarely prayed, not counting the moments before an exam. My relationship with God was much like the relationship of an ordinary person with an ambulance, say. You rarely thought of it, but boy, when you did need it, it was always a life-threatening situation.

Perhaps because the doctors at AIIMS were good, or perhaps because my prayers were powerful, I am happy to report that Balwan Singh survived. He was told to take complete rest and watch his diet. No alcohol or smoking, said the doctor. I wondered if that meant BS would stop doing his 'exercises' with Nasha, and then quickly banished the thought.

Balwan Singh went back to Balwanpur and spent the next three months at home. Every morning Sobti would go to his place with a bunch of papers that needed his signature, and return after thirty minutes. Rohan, Kabir, Nasha and I were bored stiff in the office. We had finished reading every file and every magazine. Some days we were reduced to chatting aimlessly, without any work to do. We missed the adrenalin rush. I prayed to God that something exciting would happen to make life more challenging.

# EIGHTEEN

Be careful what you wish for – it just might come true. God heard my prayers again. Three weeks after Balwan Singh left for Balwanpur, Sobti landed up in our office unannounced. He called an emergency meeting with Rohan, Kabir, Nasha and me.

When we had all gathered around in the conference room, Sobti lit his cigar and cleared his throat before he started, 'I have some difficult news for you. Balwan Singh has sold Balwanpur Industries to an American MNC. We will now be part of the famous Gronier Corporation – pronounced "Grow Near". The transition will take place in a phased manner. Over the next twelve months the takeover will be complete. As things stand, they will send a team of consultants from Brady, Adel and Smith who will study all aspects of our business. This is a time of great change and you are privileged to be the chosen ones who will be working with the consultants to manage this takeover. So the first good news is that your jobs are safe. The bad news is that we cannot say the same for many others in Balwanpur Industries. Speaking for myself,

I have decided to retire before I am asked to quit by the goras. Any questions?'

I was the first to break the long silence.

'When do these consultants start? What do we need to do to prepare?' I asked.

'Nasha, please hand over every piece of paper in Balwan Singh's office to me. I would appreciate it if you guys could help as well.' Sobti was taking charge and I noticed he did not answer my question.

So, that afternoon, we sifted through and packed all kinds of papers and documents into brown Balwanpur Industries cartons. Tucked away in a cupboard I found two albums of photographs, which Nasha snatched away and put into a separate carton that was meant for her. There was a large liquor cabinet in the office, with eighty-nine bottles of wine and four rows of bottles containing alcohol and liqueur from every corner of the world. Sobti told us we could have these. We were delighted, of course, but the mood was sombre and there was no point whistling just because I had 'inherited' sixty-eight bottles of alcohol (Nasha did not want any, so Rohan, Kabir and I had more bottles to take away as part of our booty). I know you will laugh at this and it was really stupid of me, but as I looked at those bottles of alcohol, I thought of Ayesha and her parents.

*Maybe I should gift Ayesha's parents these bottles and in return ask them to convince Ayesha to give me a divorce so that I can carry on with my life.*

*That would be a good variation on the Food for Work scheme. The Booze for Bachelorhood programme.*

I felt sorry for Nasha. She was clearly the worst hit by the news. She was very quiet as she worked, and once or twice I thought I heard her sob.

*Surely she can find another job. Maybe I should tell her that I could help her find one. I could speak to my MIJ batchmates.*

That evening, as we carted the alcohol back to our apartments, I asked Nasha if she was okay. She shook her head, and opened the door of her apartment. I ignored her protests and picked up the three heavy cartons in which she had packed the photo albums among other things and carried them all the way up to her apartment.

Nasha's eyes were red and she was sniffing from all that crying. It was strange to see her this way. I had only seen the supremely confident and upbeat side of her. I guess one's business card does make up a large part of one's self-image – if one allows it to.

She gave me a hug and said, 'Thanks Abbey, just push these into the next room. I'll unpack tomorrow. I won't be going back to that office ever again. Please say goodbye to Rohan and Kabir for me and tell them I'll miss all the fun we had, working together.'

I took the heaviest carton and groaned as I carried it into what looked like Nasha's bedroom. It was tastefully done up and everything was neatly in place. On her dressing table was a picture of Sobti and a woman who looked strangely familiar. For the life of me I couldn't remember where I had met her. I turned back to see Nasha standing at the door.

'What are you doing with Captain's photo in your bedroom?' I asked the obvious question.

She looked at me for a moment, then seemed to come to some sort of a decision. 'He is my father. That's my mother next to him. You probably know her as Mrs Sohanlal Negi,' Nasha said very quietly.

I was too stunned to react. Nasha told me the whole story then, in short, abbreviated sentences, her tone emotionless: Captain Sobti had invited Sohanlal and his wife to his house for dinner – Negi had just taken over as the leader of the workers' union and was negotiating a wage increase on behalf of the workers. Negi had got drunk, and Captain Sobti had taken advantage of his wife. That's when Nasha was conceived. Sobti sent Negi's wife away for a year. Nasha was educated at a girls' school in Simla. After finishing school, she got into Miranda House, in Delhi University. The day she finished college, there was a job waiting for her in the Chairman's office.

'I hate that bastard, Sobti,' Nasha summarized.

'I can understand that, but at the end of the day he is your father,' I consoled her.

'What kind of a father hands over his daughter to the Chairman to be his mistress?' Nasha enquired.

'Is that why some factory workers tried to kill Captain Sobti? I remember Dr Pat telling me about it.'

'Yes, Negi and his men assaulted Sobti with iron rods. They beat him till they thought he was dead. He survived because Dr Patronobish happened to be driving by and saw him lying there in a pool of blood. I hate him for being my father. I hate him because he has ruined my mother's life and mine. I go down to the factory every year on the annual sports day so that I can see my mother among the spectators. Why should I have to put up with this façade? It bothers me to see Sobti in the office and pretend that he is just another employee of the company. I still don't know how he managed to make peace with Negi and why Negi and my mother continue to live in Balwanpur – maybe I'm better off not knowing!'

I got her a glass of water. Then I moved the other two cartons into her bedroom, sweating with the effort. My shirt was all creased and dirty. I needed a shower. I gave Nasha a hug and told her it was time for me to go and that she should call me if she needed anything. That's when the doorbell rang. We looked at each other and wondered who could possibly be visiting her at this hour. It was 10:45 p.m.

I was right behind Nasha as she opened the door. It was Keya. She looked at me in that dishevelled state, her eyes wide.

'Oh, hi Keya. This is Nasha, my colleague. I was helping her with some stuff that she brought in from the office today. It was her last day at work,' I said.

'So you were giving her a farewell present. I can see it was real hard work,' Keya said as she turned and left.

I ran after her, but she didn't stop or talk to me.

'Keya! Listen to me… Please don't do this… Keya!' I pleaded as she ran down the stairs.

I tried to grab her elbow as she left the apartment complex. She wriggled out of my reach and blindly ran across the road. I made to go after her, but one step was all I managed. The next thing I knew, I was knocked off my feet and flying through the air. Before my body could hit the ground again, I blacked out.

# NINETEEN

I woke up feeling fuzzy. I tried to move but couldn't. I looked up and tried to speak but my throat was parched. I heard familiar voices.

'Baba, Ma, Bhai has regained consciousness.' Asmita's voice sounded clear and happy.

Baba chided me softly, 'Chotka, you are so careless. Don't you know that you should watch out for traffic before you cross a busy street…'

'Of course he knows how to cross the road. It is these car drivers who drive so carelessly. It's thanks to God that Chotka has survived. I have to go now, to the Kali temple. Come, let's go.' Ma dragged my father away and Asmita reluctantly followed them out.

Then I heard Keya's voice. 'Abbey, I am sorry. I am so sorry. How can I even apologize for my stupidity? Please forgive me. Does it hurt still? You got five stitches just below your lip. Gosh!'

That comment made me smile and immediately, I grimaced in pain. I looked around the room and spoke in sign language to Nasha and Keya, enquiring about what had happened.

Keya said, 'You were hit by a speeding car. The impact threw you onto the footpath. That's what saved you, actually. If you had fallen on the road, the next vehicle would have crushed you. I turned back when I heard the screech of the car. You were lying senseless on the pavement. Luckily, Mr Samtani from the Railway Colony, who happened to be in a car just behind, recognized you and brought you to the Railway Hospital in CP.'

I pointed to Nasha and gesticulated, trying to tell Keya that nothing had happened between Nasha and me that evening.

Nasha sat next to me and said, 'When Keya walked away and you ran after her, I realized what she must have thought. I followed you but you guys must have been running like crazy. I reached the accident spot minutes after it happened. I am sorry I was the cause of all this. I truly am sorry, Abbey.'

'You've been unconscious for three days. Your mother didn't move from your side for one moment. Nasha and I kept telling her to go back home, but she was adamant.'

'Yesterday the MIJ gang was here to meet you. They are really nice people,' said Nasha.

Keya added, 'Yeah, Pappu, Gur, Joy, Arunesh and Neetika were here. They all look so different now. They have left a huge bouquet for you. There was also a surprise visitor for you – Father Hathaway. Didn't he teach you at MIJ? He is such a handsome man, just like Gregory Peck.

All the girls in the BEd college used to swoon over his good looks, but you guys called him Haathi, didn't you? He is very fond of you, Abbey. He stood here muttering his prayers and left this envelope for you.'

I opened the envelope, which was simply marked 'For Abbey'. Inside was a small card made by an NGO that supports the educational efforts of slum children. Haathi had inscribed on it, in his unmistakable, neat handwriting:

> Dear Abbey,
>
> I heard about your accident when I came to Delhi on work yesterday. Get well soon – there is so much to be done to make this world a better place, you can't possibly waste time in hospital.
>
> We have already started planning for the reunion of the batch of 1984. We will be contacting you for sponsorships. We have also started work on some expansion programmes at MIJ. When you come next, you will see how pretty your alma mater is looking.
>
> My warmest regards,
>
> Ed Hathaway

The nurse came and announced the end of visiting hours. I tried to tell Nasha and Keya that they should go home, but my words came out so weird, I switched to dumb charades. They turned to leave the room and then Keya came back.

She whispered in my ear, 'Abbey, I hope the stitches

won't cramp your style too much. I miss being kissed. I love you. Get well soon.'

I was discharged from the hospital after a week. Baba and Ma wouldn't listen to my protests and took me home. Ma took it upon herself to make sure every drop of blood that I had lost in the accident was instantly made up. The only problem was that the stitches made eating painful. It was even more difficult to smoke.

I lay in bed trying to read a book of poems by Pritish Nandy. Keya had scribbled on the first page of the book: 'Love and best wishes for a million shared sunrises, Keya.'

Ma came in with a bowl of chicken soup and sat next to me. Keya's handwriting was clearly legible even from that distance.

Ma gave a fleeting glance at the book and said in a matter-of-fact tone, 'You really love Keya, don't you? I like her. She seems like a nice girl. You need to get your divorce, though. How long will the two of you stay apart?' She leaned closer. 'Your stitches are drying well. But I think the scar will remain.'

'Ma, stop worrying about me. I am fine. The scar will remind me that I need to be careful while crossing the road. Keya is a nice girl – just a bit crazy and unpredictable at times.' I nearly confided in my mother then, my doubts about our relationship. And what others said about her. None of my friends ever said it out loud, but I knew they thought of her as melodramatic, flighty, weird, pretentious. My favourite, and much kinder, word for the girl I loved was: high-maintenance.

'She and that other girl from your office stayed up all night with me in the hospital. They were both praying for your recovery. At one point I was worried that they would need medical attention themselves.'

Asmita came into the room. 'Bhai, there is a call for you from Dubai. Mr Rustom Topiwalla is on the line.'

Ma left the room and took Asmita along so that she could not eavesdrop.

'Hello, Rusty! What a surprise. What's up? Do you know that Balwanpur is going to be a part of...'

'Gronier Corporation. I know. And Brady, Adel and Smith is going to help in the transition. I knew about it when you were asking me all those questions about doing fancy stuff in HR. Actually, I know people in the Chicago office of Brady. The Brady part of the firm is Sophie Ann Brady. She's an MBA from Harvard, and she's a hot blonde who is into yoga, Hinduism and Indian cuisine in a big way. You need to charm your way into her good books.'

'That's useful to know, Rusty. I am sure it will be nice to have a hot blonde in the office. Is she single and ready to mingle? Hey, Rusty, have you ever slept with a blonde? I'd love to find out if they are as good in bed as they're supposed to be.'

Rusty ignored my query and instead offered a crash course in cultural sensitivity, 'Americans are different from Indians. Please remember that, unlike us, they do not socialize in the office, so limit your office interaction to business and don't try and make her room some old-fashioned adda. Asking Sophie about her family, etc., may seem to her more like an intrusion of privacy than a friendly gesture. Wait for her to offer that information. When she asks about your family, be brief and say that your parents and sister live in Delhi. Don't get into elaborate details about where your father works and all that. The thumb rule with Yanks is, avoid showing your emotions. You are very punctual – that's great. Most Indians don't get it. They don't understand that being late for a meeting is not done when you are working with non-Indians. Brief the others in your office as well. One last thing – when you are invited for a business dinner or lunch, the prime objective is not the food but the networking. That's when you can swap stories, etc.'

'Damn it. why is life getting so complicated? With so many dos and don'ts to worry about, I often wonder why I should continue to slave away in some shitty organization. Maybe I should become an entrepreneur? Not that I know what sort of business to get into. How does one start a company that is guaranteed to succeed? I guess the trick is to make a product that everyone uses – rich and poor, old and young, men and women, rural and urban…' I finally said what had been at the back of my mind for a long time.

Rascal Rusty, as always, had an ingenious solution to the problem. 'There's the germ of a business proposition in Scott Fitzgerald's famous line: "The rich get richer and the poor get – children." Abbey, take my advice and get into the business of selling condoms. That's the only product that fits the demographic profile you are talking about –

rich and poor, old and young, men and women, rural and urban. It's a million-dollar idea. Go for it, Abbey!'

'I'll have to find a nifty name for it. How about Highway Rubbers?' I suggested.

'The best name for a condom in India would be "Dipper". Every truck on the highway will automatically advertise it. Haven't you noticed the slogan "Use Dipper at Night"? It's painted on the back of most trucks.'

'We can differentiate the products by calling them Dipper Premium for the rich, Dipper Regular for the middle-class and Dipper Lite for the poor. Hey, thanks, glad we spoke about this. By the way, I meant to ask you something. I believe you gave Vishy the idea that he should become a religious leader of sorts. Neats told me about the ashram he runs in Tamil Nadu. How come you never suggest such great ideas to me?' I said in a mock serious tone.

'Starting a religious sect is an eternal fallback option. Vishy wanted to opt out of the corporate rat race and decided to try my formula earlier than usual – but it works. Look, every religion must answer three basic questions: (a) How did I come to the earth in this shape and form? (b) Where will I go after I die? (c) While I am on earth, how can my troubles be minimized and how can I be happy? You could formulate your answers in exactly the same way we used to write term papers at MIJ. You could go to the library, read the reference books and then create an answer that's the amalgamation of all those books. Similarly, read up the holy books of a few major religions and then create your version that liberally draws from all these. Or else, you create your hypothesis and go ahead and build a convincing logic around it. In fact, in religion you could always say my hypothesis comes from the conversation I had with God, and you'll be home.' Rusty spoke as though he had anticipated my question.

My head was buzzing with ideas. 'Rusty, I saw Vishy's photo. He was wearing a sky blue robe and had long hair and a beard.'

Rusty said, 'The clothing and hairstyle are part of the packaging and branding. That is what helps you market your version of religion. Remember I told you in MIJ that you need to think about packaging after you've written a term paper? Just great content might get you a B plus, but packaging and presentation move it beyond. By adding graphs and pictures, you can move your grade from B plus to an A or an A plus. When you start your own religious sect, you can choose to brand yourself and your followers in any way that makes them different. In fact, to attract more followers, you should allow your followers to do all that they have been told not to do, or do with feelings of guilt. Hey, maybe your sect should tell people to wear blue jeans and white T-shirts with a logo of the sect. That would be unique. You will make it easy for the school- and college-going crowd to sign up. All those who feel they look young enough to carry off such clothes will also join you. On a different note, now that you are part of Gronier Corporation, maybe you should corporatize religion. You could easily be the CEO of that division.'

He concluded with a hearty chuckle and said, 'I almost forgot why I called. The MIJ circuit is buzzing with the news that you had the accident because you were literally chasing your old flame from the campus days – that girl from the BEd class... What was her name... Keya, right? Good for you, Abbey. Wish you a speedy recovery. I am very happy for you. Even though Ayesha is a friend, I still say whatever she did to you was wrong. Is there any chance of your coming to Dubai, by the way?'

'I am hoping you'll send me an air ticket. You stingy bastard, you are the one who's working for the sheikhs. Thanks for calling, Rusty. Bye.' I hung up before he could get into any more talk about Keya.

# TWENTY

I went to the office after six weeks. The stitches had healed, but the prominent scar below my lip served as a reminder of that evening when I almost lost Keya, and my life. There was still a slight trace of a limp in my right leg, which I was very conscious of. The doctor had assured me that it would disappear in about four weeks if I followed the prescribed exercise routine. Ma and Baba came to drop me back to my apartment. Asmita helped me clean up the place and half an hour later, it looked good and smelled fresh again.

The office looked and felt different without Balwan Singh in his corner room. The buzz was missing. So were Rohan and Kabir. They had decided to start a boutique consulting firm in Bombay. They had left a note on my table with their new phone number and contacts and with an open invitation to join their firm should I ever decide to quit Balwanpur Industries – sorry, the Gronier Corporation. I looked at the note and smiled as I thought of the good times we had had together. I missed having them around.

The new stationery with the insignia of Gronier Corporation arrived the same afternoon. The name of Balwanpur Industries was systematically being erased from every place. It felt as though we were disowning our past. The business cards and letterheads were just the beginning. A marketing campaign had been created by our new ad agency, Norihito and Daifu. It was called 'Come Closer' and they had invited all the vice presidents to the presentation. To demonstrate the concept, the creative team came into the office together, each with an arm around a colleague. Their presenters (two hot looking babes) were also joined at the hip with a large oversized belt. It was such a distraction. I kept imagining them doing all sorts of unprintable stuff. Increasingly, advertising seemed like an attractive career option. Who knew what one could get away with in the name of 'offbeat ideas' and 'challenging convention'?

Eighty-eight slides and seven short commercials later, they had worn down our defences and convinced us that their strategy was the best and that we should cough up the funds for the campaign.

'The world is coming closer. The super on top of the logo will say: Gronier Corporation – making the world a global community for twenty years. We are getting the people to see the word Gronier as GROW-NEAR, get the strategy? We want to own the word "closer",' said Tahira, the Client Servicing Director.

The furniture was being replaced and the office was being expanded. The Gronier Corporation offices now occupied three floors of the building. The cleaning staff and the office peon Saryu Nath had left – they were asked to go, and were given a lump sum so that they would go peacefully. We were all expected to fetch our own tea or coffee from the vending machines in the little kitchenette. The consultants were to come in and spend the next few weeks studying the factory. Since Sobti had also quit, I was left as the only link with the past. I had not met Captain since that fateful day when Nasha told me about her parentage. I was overcome by a sense of disgust each time I thought of him.

Sophie Ann Brady arrived in the office that evening with three suitcases full of papers and books. A room had been booked for her at the Taj – a privilege associated only with the Chairman in the past. She was dressed in a formal business suit and looked like she was barely into her thirties. She had the bluest of blue eyes, and a somewhat husky voice. She parked herself in what was earlier Rohan's office cubicle and rearranged things to suit herself. I noticed she had a photograph of herself with two young kids. She seemed to feel at home in the new space already.

I walked in and introduced myself.

'Hi Abbey! I am Sophie Ann Brady, just call me Sophie. I lead the Human Capital Practice for our firm. I believe you and I are supposed to be leading this project on resource optimisation options for Gronier. I am looking forward to working with you. So tell me about yourself.'

I summarized my life in three minutes and noticed

that Sophie had this thing about taking notes. If any human being on the planet spoke in her presence, she noted down the words. She also had a set of phrases that struck me as... well... different. For example, this bit about human capital. I wanted to ask if that was the same as human resources. I had just got out of saying personnel management.

I wanted to ask her about the two children whose photo was so prominently displayed, but refrained. Rusty's advice was still fresh in my mind.

At exactly 5:30 p.m., Sophie switched off the lights in her office and asked if I would join her for a drink. Rusty had said that dinner meetings were networking opportunities. I wasn't sure if going for a drink constituted the same. Maybe it did. So I tagged along and joined her at the restaurant in the Taj. Now was the time to discuss personal stuff.

I opened the conversation after we had clinked glasses. 'Cheers! How long have you been married?'

Sophie almost choked in surprise. 'Why do you want to know that?'

'Don't tell me if you don't want to, Sophie. I was just being polite. I saw the picture of the two kids on your table. That's why I thought... you might be missing them...' I felt like an ass for starting off on the wrong note and cursed Rascal Rusty for not warning me.

'Relax, Abbey, I have no problem telling you about them. I was just a bit unprepared for the question, that's all. They are my brother's kids. They were with me last summer. Before you ask me the next question, let me tell you. I am not married. I had a boyfriend when I was in Harvard, but he did not want to leave Wall Street and I wanted to see the world. So we broke up. I read somewhere that in India people like to know all about you. Now I know it's true.'

I told Sophie about Ayesha and how she was now in New York, running Mystical Dreams. After a moment's hesitation, I told her that we were separated. She mentioned how she had been reading about the rising incidence of divorce in urban India. I wondered if I should tell her about Keya and then decided to save it for another day.

The next morning Sophie told me that she had had a long chat with Matt about his expectations from the project. It took me a second to recall that Matt possibly meant Matt Keller, our new CEO. One of the expectations was that I would accompany Sophie to the factory at Balwanpur and help her with the project. A month later, we would present our recommendations to Matt and the new board of directors.

Since I was now the de-facto head of HR of Balwanpur Industries/Gronier Corporation, I thought it would be a good opportunity for me to find out how things were at the factory. We had been in a state of limbo for a while. I was not sure whether I was meant to be taking over from Sobti, or if I should wait for someone to tell me that I was in charge. I remembered what Rusty had once said to me: If someone had to be told to take charge, that in itself meant the person was not ready to be a leader.

Sophie and I went to the factory and she instantly started to make elaborate notes on the number of people in each section and the number of grades, and what the per employee productivity was, etc. She had a zillion figures scribbled in her notes and would spend the evenings creating tables and charts that she drew herself. She was a stickler for time. She would start work at 8:30 a.m. and spend the first hour writing down what she meant to accomplish during the day. In the evening, at 4:30 p.m., she would be back in the office for an hour, organizing her information under various headings. At 5:30 sharp, she would close shop. She never worked on a Saturday or Sunday.

It was good to be back in the factory. I spent time with the workers in every section. Negi invited me home. His wife had made jalebis for me. As I ate, I wondered if she ever missed Nasha. Now that Nasha was without a job, would she get a chance to come to the factory to meet her mother?

Sohanlal Negi told me that the Irulas were getting restless and were trying to form a new union. He recommended that I get Arai falsely implicated in a police case and get him locked up.

Negi confided to me, 'There have been so many occasions when Captain Sobti asked me to get someone out of the factory by getting them into a police case. The local Superintendent of Police, Qureshi, is a very close friend of his. You can leave it to me. I just need your go-ahead.'

'We will not do anything that is unethical, Negi. Captain Sobti may have chosen to do things in a certain way. I have my own methods. I will not use falsehood in my dealings. Let me talk to Arai and find out what is bothering him,' I told Negi firmly.

I drove down to the Irula village the following day and met Arai. He was sitting under a tree, teaching some children. The children saw me first and kept pointing at me as I stood beside them, trying to catch Arai's attention. Eventually he looked up and saw me. We shook hands.

'Arai, I came to meet you and find out how things have been with you. Where is Daya?' I asked.

'Daya has gone to Chennai to join an English-medium school. He is very happy there. It is much better being among your own. The Irulas here are very unhappy. Our children do not get free education in the schools run by the company. And we cannot afford to pay. Does that mean our children will be denied something that is fundamental to every individual?'

I said impulsively, 'Arai, I will instruct the schools of our township to admit one child per Irula family. We will bear the fee for that child. But what is this I hear about another union?'

Arai stared at me, trying to gauge my intentions before responding. 'It is not the workers who form a union, it is the poor practices of the management that instigate the workers. When we heard that the company had been sold, we thought it was in our interest to form a really strong and independent union that was not led by corrupt people like Negi. Some of the younger workers are disillusioned with the existing union, which they feel is a puppet union. They wanted me to lead the group. Are you disappointed that I am doing so?'

'Arai, I am happy that you are representing the people. I still remember that you gave away the five thousand rupees that I had given you when you brought in that cobra. It is rare to find a leader who puts his people first. I am sure it will do them a lot of good. All I'd like to say to you is, do not form a second union in the company. That never helps. Instead, if you feel you have the people's support, let them elect you in place of Negi.' I looked Arai straight in the eye as I spoke.

That evening I joined Sophie at the club. She was having her usual Scotch on the rocks. We got talking about the factory.

'Abbey, why is it that every Indian company has this paternalistic style of management? The Balwanpur factory has a cradle-to-condom welfare policy. Isn't that bad business practice?'

'Is being paternalistic and welfare-oriented bad business practice?' I asked.

'When you look at a country like India where there is little or no social security provided by the state, the role of the employer and the expectations from the employer get heightened. The question to ask ourselves is, what business are we in? Why are we in the business of running this township, for instance? If a worker's house needs repairs, it becomes the obligation of the company to fix it. Why is that so? Isn't it a bad business model?'

'Why is it not wrong that the company reimburses the entertainment expenses of the managers? Why should the company pay the directors' electricity bills? That is what I call a bad business model,' I said.

'I agree. The world is changing. India will soon become a global player. It will then have to play beyond its comfort zones. This company has been bled dry already. Its products are overpriced because of the high cost of labour. We will need to automate. The workers need to embrace new technology including computerization to become competitive.'

Sophie had worked in many countries in Southeast Asia before she arrived to take up this assignment in India. While in Singapore and Malaysia, she had spent three years studying Indian life and culture. She had a great interest in Indian cuisine and yoga, courtesy her stint in Chicago. Sometimes it seemed that she was in love with India.

Sophie said to me one evening, 'Each one of the states of India has a different cuisine. From appetizers to dessert, it is all different. Isn't that amazing? I realized after coming here that there is no such thing as Indian cuisine. There isn't a single dish that is common to every state.' She added, 'I have cooked chicken curry and Indian bread for dinner. There is some kheer too, though it hasn't turned out as well as I'd hoped. But what the hell, life is all about trying. Do you want to join me, Abbey?'

Mrs Dayal had made me swear that I would go to her place for dinner. She wanted to update me on all the gossip. So I told Sophie that I would join her another evening.

Mrs Dayal asked me within minutes of our meeting, 'Have you filed for a divorce yet, or does Ayesha want to come back?'

'Ayesha is happy running her own boutique in New York. That's what she has always wanted to do. And I am happy here. So, to answer your question, Mrs Dayal, yes, I do want to file for a divorce, if that is what Ayesha wants as well, but it's better done when Ayesha is here, even if it is for a few hours, to sign the papers.'

'Who would have thought that Ayesha would do something so immature? She is so selfish. She has not divorced you, just so you can't marry again. That is so unfair.'

'Let's talk about other things. Where is Funtoosh?' I asked.

Mrs Dayal had tears in her eyes as she replied, 'My baby Funtoosh has left Mummy all alone. He died two months back. My little beta had kidney failure. He suffered so much, and none of the doctors in Balwanpur could help.'

The lights in Balwanpur seemed dimmer. The people seemed down. The grass in the lawn looked dusty. The old sparkle was gone. Everyone seemed uncertain about their future.

I spoke to Sophie the next evening about my observations. She said it was to be expected. The organization would need to be shepherded through this transition. A change of guard was never easy for the employees or the employers to manage.

'What can we do to get this place to be vibrant and enthusiastic again? It hurts me to see everyone looking so defeated. They never expected that Balwan Singh would sell out,' I said.

Sophie's eyes reflected a passing flicker of anger as she said, 'Your adored Chairman has treated this company like his personal fiefdom. There have been no investments in computerization or in skill-building for the future. A leader is judged by how well he or she has been able to build the capability of the people.' She picked up her bag and stood. 'I am going home to do some work on my presentation. It has been such a stressful day.'

'I agree that we need to computerize. That's the way forward. May I see what you are presenting to the board?' I was curious to see how the Harvard MBA would put together a roadmap for the future.

'Sure,' said Sophie. 'Come along. You can stay for dinner too, if you like.'

Once we were ensconced in her study, Sophie gathered up a sheaf of papers. There were drawings of the factory layout and equipment on neat white sheets of paper, done in jet-black ink. There was a bunch marked 'As Is' and another marked 'To Be'. There were annotations explaining assumptions and hypotheses. The financial impact of the proposal was in a separate section. I pored over the numbers and then went to the portions marked 'Strictly confidential'.

Sophie opened her liquor cabinet and pulled out a bottle of Old Monk. She had a bottle of Jamaican rum in the other hand. I voted in favour of Old Monk.

Sophie laughed as she poured the drinks. 'I knew you would choose this. It has certainly earned a permanent place in my bar. I've decided I must carry a few cases of Old Monk for colleagues back home in Chicago. And whenever I run out, you'll have to find a way to get two bottles to the US for me.'

'That's not a problem. I'll run the supply chain for you as part of my plan to build cross-functional experience. But listen, you have recommended computerization in the office and automation in so many sections of our manufacturing process – wouldn't that mean loss of jobs for our employees? What do we do to find jobs for those employees who will be rendered surplus?' I took a generous sip of the familiar OM2 concoction.

'That's a good question, and do you know what a good question is? A question that has no answer – at least not one that we can come up with tonight!' Sophie laughed.

'But isn't that something we need to think of before we pull the plug?'

'I don't think Gronier will get rid of everyone at once. It may happen over the next three or four years. I have not recommended a timeframe within which it needs to be done. That will depend on your ability to manage the change through the many rounds of communication and counselling. I think you will figure out something, Abbey. I think you are smart and care for the employees. But you need to work with your head as well as your heart. A consultant is hired to provide the best solution the head can come up with. The managers need to implement it by using their heart. I have seen you talking to the workers here. You have a great amount of credibility. Use that.'

She smiled then, and walked off to get some more ice and another bag of American potato chips. She said over her shoulder, 'Abbey, will you please stop talking shop? A consultant's services are billed by the hour, so there is no free advice for you. Plenty of other things could be free, but not advice.'

I thought of the employees of Balwanpur. They trusted me. I had to figure out a way of not letting them down. Maybe they should get computer friendly and thus become a part of the change. It wasn't going to be easy, I knew. How would we get people who had all kinds of apprehensions about computerization to actually embrace the technology? But at least I now knew the end point; I just had to find a way to get there.

*Sophie is rather attractive, isn't she? Look at those deep blue eyes and the husky voice... quite a turn on.*

*Look at that shapely body. I wonder what she looks like naked.*

*What about Keya?*

*You forget, my friend, that I am not married to Keya, I am married to Ayesha. Technically speaking, if anybody has the right to object to my being married but available, it is Ayesha.*

*Maybe if Ayesha knows that you slept with Sophie, she will go ahead and divorce you. That would be a perfect example of mixing business with pleasure.*

*There is a greater chance of her divorcing me if she knows that I am now with Keya.*

*Naah... she has already had the satisfaction of taking Keya away from you. It doesn't matter any longer. Being married is a tag that Ayesha can leverage to her advantage whenever she wants.*

I was filled with a deep disgust and hatred towards Ayesha. I could not marry Keya, nor could I sleep with Sophie without feeling guilty.

Sophie came back with the ice pail and two bags of chips. She had changed into a pair of khakis and a printed cotton top. I could smell perfume on her. She sat down next to me and passed me the chips.

We sat in silence for a while and I finished my third drink. I put the glass down and told Sophie that I needed to leave before I got completely drunk. She took my hand in hers and said playfully, 'You can leave in the morning, when you are sober again.'

Without thinking, I cupped her face with my hands. Then I allowed my fingers to trail down to her breasts. She had made it easy for me by removing her top. Her face lifted to mine and she brought her lips close for a kiss.

Something was happening to me. It must be the alcohol. A minute ago, Sophie was this naked goddess I was going to spend the night with. The next minute, when I looked at her, all I saw was the cold-blooded person who had recommended that the majority of the five thousand workers of Balwanpur should be laid off as part of the process of not 'downsizing' but 'right sizing'. This was crazy. Here was my chance to live my fantasy of making love to a blonde. Instead, all I could see was a manipulative human being. It felt as though I was getting ready to fuck a serial killer. I did the dumbest thing then. I gave Sophie a light hug and walked back to my room in the guesthouse, a tad unsteady on my feet.

The English language does have different words to describe a friend and a colleague. It doesn't have a word for a colleague with whom one can also have sex. I guess that in itself is meant to be a warning – keep your pants zipped when you are with colleagues.

## TWENTY-ONE

My relationship with Sophie was never the same after that night. We came back to Delhi the next day and spent another week working on the presentation that was now scheduled for Tuesday. I wasn't sure if I should initiate a conversation with her about what had happened. I took care not to be alone in the room with her in case she raised the matter. And I ensured that I didn't touch her, even accidentally, though I felt quite stupid behaving this way.

One evening, Sophie got up, shut the door of her office and faced me with her hands on her hips. I knew this was the moment. I shot off a silent prayer to God, giving him a general power of attorney to save my life.

Sophie looked at me and said, 'Abbey, will you stop making an ass of yourself? If you continue your touch-me-not act for another day, the whole office will be buzzing with rumour and speculation about what happened between us. I like you and I still do. You told me that you and Ayesha are separated and that she was in New York. You never mentioned being in a relationship.

So I presumed you were unattached and asked you over – that's something I have never done with a colleague. I even felt I could invite you to stay over. You chose not to and I... really, I respect that. We don't always have to like everyone who likes us. We can still be friends, can't we? I am sorry I made you uncomfortable. Can you please now forget about that evening and behave normally? Please?'

I felt sorry for her. I had thought I was behaving in an exemplary fashion by exercising supreme verbal restraint. I wanted to tell her I hadn't meant to reject her. I wanted to tell her that I had lost track of the many occasions when I had been snubbed by a girl. If she was Indian, I might have said all that I wanted to, but this was a firangi chick and there was no need to display any emotion, as Rusty had warned me. So I listened to her with an expressionless face and promised her I would behave normally.

*What does she mean when she says I should be seen to be behaving normally?*

*Maybe now I should actively start pawing her to display a deep sense of comfort.*

But there was definitely a thaw in our relationship. Later that evening, after spending the rest of the day working on the presentation, I told Sophie I was sick of making transparencies and putting data from rows into columns and vice versa. I had already made pie charts and presented bar graphs of data, each time with a different scale to make sure they looked dramatic enough.

Sophie said to me, 'Having good presentation skills is the secret to success in the corporate world. Beyond a certain level in the organization, the ability to put forth a complicated thought in a simple manner gives people proof of superior leadership skills. Abbey, you have to get better at this in order to get ahead in your career.'

I agreed. 'I thought I had finished writing term papers and doing presentations when I left MIJ. You know, at MIJ, a slick presentation could make the difference between an A and an A plus. That's why a couple of my batchmates were always in demand, to make presentations on behalf of other students. Isn't it weird, during one's work life, everything other than work impacts your life. So it is not just your professional calibre but your ability to make small talk, choose the right wine, make the right golfing buddies and all that jazz which determines how high you get up the business ladder. Captain Sobti would have described this as the law of paradoxes. The higher you want to go, the more you have to lower yourself.'

'That's true, Abbey. Though you shouldn't look at it only negatively. It could also mean that the more ambitious you are and the more intent you are on climbing the corporate ladder, the more you need to keep in mind the interests of those at the bottom of the pyramid.' Sophie interpreted that one brilliantly.

D-day finally arrived. Sophie and I had been working as though possessed. This would be my first interaction with Matt Keller and the board. I had worn a jacket, a white shirt and a tie as advised by Sophie. Keya had sent me a small swab of cotton sprayed with her perfume as a reminder that she was with me.

I had called Rascal Rusty a few days ago for some last-minute advice. He told me that smelling one's favourite perfume while reading up facts and figures helps the mind to store them better. All you had to do was smell the perfume once again, and you would recall everything. I tried the trick at least twenty times until I was convinced that it was indeed effective. A lingering doubt remained whether the credit for my memorizing those numbers should go to the trick Rusty had taught me or to my superior capability.

Matt Keller turned out to be a fit forty-five-year-old who had represented his college at basketball and football. I shook hands with him and the rest of the board members, then took up position at the head of the room. I had put all my slides in order and rehearsed the opening lines and some key facts and figures. I had dabbed my shirt cuff with the aftershave lotion that was to serve as a mnemonic device. Now, I discreetly smelt the cuff and was about to launch into my spiel when Matt Keller cleared his throat. I waited for him to speak.

He looked at the others and said, 'If it's okay with everyone, let's just discuss the proposal rather than look at transparencies.'

Everybody nodded except me. I was caught completely off-guard. I had not anticipated this approach. I joined the group at the table and spread out my slides in front of me. Without the solace of the slides, I was a nervous wreck. Each question seemed to throw me deeper into confusion and soon I was stammering and stuttering. I was recommending investment in training, in providing the workmen with computer skills so that they would remain employable. Matt Keller (the smart-aleck sod had played offence during his football days) kept asking why we needed to worry about keeping workmen employable. We got into a debate on the role of the new management and the expectations the workmen had from the new team. Matt was getting more and more aggressive. The other board members were also jumping into the slippery arena. I don't know why, but I thought of Father Hathaway's line: 'There are three sides to an argument – your side, my side and the facts.' I was about to use that when I saw Sophie raise her hand. She had been a mute spectator to my humiliation.

She stepped up to the front of the room and addressed the group. 'Good morning. I have rarely seen a board that is so clued in and engaged. It's a great debate we have had so far, and very energizing. But, as they say, if everything is going well, it simply means that we have overlooked something. So, while I must thank you for all the great ideas you have put across, let us just revisit the objectives of our presentation this morning. It would help in the discussion if I could show the details on a slide so that we are all on the same page. We could go through the facts using the transparencies and then after we have all made our notes regarding the data, we could switch off the projector and work out an action plan, after which we agree on the timelines for implementing it.'

The preamble was awesome. It pacified all the vampires on the board and had them nodding and smiling again.

Sophie made eye contact with each board member and with Matt before stating, 'The objective of our presentation today is to establish how to enhance the profitability of the Gronier Corporation. The strategy would be to enhance the automation level and the tactical response would be to build computer literacy of the operators on the shopfloor.'

Matt Keller leaned back in his chair and smiled like a proud father showing off his favourite child. The others nodded as if to acknowledge that they were in safe hands. Sophie demonstrated how each step would impact profits. When she was done, she turned away from the screen and invited questions. Matt was the first to raise his hand. How could we create a campaign that would generate enthusiasm among the workers, he wanted to know.

Sophie looked at me for a second and said, 'Before I answer that, I want to thank Abbey, whose insights and deep analyses helped us to craft the vision that I have just shared. As you saw, he played the difficult role of building the engagement of the board on the issue and pre-soaked your minds before I presented the plan of resource optimization for the corporation. He and his team are busy giving finishing touches to a communication plan to create a pull-factor for the workers in the factory. We will run the campaign past Matt and align him before we execute it.'

The meeting was over. The board members thanked Sophie and me for doing such an awesome job. I was thankful to Sophie for saving the day. When everyone had left, I pulled her aside to express my appreciation.

'Why is it that when I said the same things you did, I got opposition from the board, whereas you got their approval? Does it have anything to do with your having the right skin colour?'

Sophie was not offended by the question, which in itself was a miracle. If someone had asked me a similar question, I would have kicked him in the teeth. Sophie just smiled.

'I started off by addressing their primary expectation from any plan – its impact on business profitability. The new board will have to show how they have impacted the profits in the first ninety days. That, of course, is a bit of an American thing – get the low hanging fruits first. You were positioning the presentation as a plan to keep the workmen employable. I looked at it as a plan to keep the company profitable. Both of us said the same thing, but one was closer to the heart of the audience. Above all, I must confess, at every stage I have been keeping Matt in the loop on my ideas and suggestions. When you spoke, he had no clue what stance you would take, so he played it safe and sided with the board. In my case, he knew what I was going to say and he could relax because he knew there would be no surprises. Hey, don't get so hassled about it. You did a great job. The board loves you.'

That evening I sat in my room practicing the art of blowing smoke rings at the ceiling. My mind kept playing back the conversation with Sophie. For the first time, I realized to what extent my work – and life – were about being a communicator.

# TWENTY-TWO

$\mathrm{A}$ week after making the presentation to Matt and the board, Sophie left for Chicago. She told me that she was planning to take a few weeks off before she took up her next assignment in China. I became quite fond of Sophie during those months we spent trying to put together a plan for the factory. This was the first time I'd had a chance to work with someone who had actually studied at the Harvard Business School.

Sophie used to say, 'At the end of the day, we are all owners of a business, not just the function we represent. Think of yourself as being an actor in a play. Your lines are important, but what is more important is that the play is successful.'

She left me wiser and certainly savvier about dealing with Matt Keller and the board. The immediate task was to get the workers excited about computerization. The Indian prime minister at this time was also trying to push for computerization. I decided to be an evangelist for the process by practicing what I preached. I ordered a brand new PC for every manager's office. The managers were less than enthusiastic about it. Ramadorai, who now headed the accounts department at the factory, was reluctant to have the machine occupy space in his office.

I spoke to Rascal Rusty about the difficulty I was having, trying to get the managers to embrace technology. Rusty thought for a minute and said that I should make it someone's full-time job.

I immediately saw the sense of that and said, 'Good thought. I will hire a Manager, Computerization for the company. That will put adequate focus on the task.'

Rusty said, 'The person should report to the CEO – that will ensure you get the best and the brightest to apply for the job. Look for a creative person rather than a technical whiz. Some of the techies can be prize morons when it comes to dealing with people. In this role, the key skill is persuasiveness rather than tech wizardry. Give the guy the designation of Vice President, Information Systems rather than Vice President, Computerization. That will lower the immediate resistance. Tell the CEO that the true worth of a chief executive can be seen in the way he deals with HR and computerization. Both need initial investments before you can start to see results. Talking of investments, look at the way the stock market in India is doing. That's where the money is going to be.'

The person I hired for the role was an engineer from IIT who had no desire to be an engineer. Gauri Swaminathan was a petite Tamil Brahmin from Madras. Thanks to her father, who had retired as a colonel in the Indian Army, she had done the 'eight different schools before I joined college' routine, like most Army kids. She spoke five languages fluently and managed a smattering of a few more. She had represented IIT at table tennis and played the violin.

Gauri set about her task with great dedication. First off all, I pointed her in the direction of Ramadorai, the greatest opponent of computerization.

'Hello, Mr Ramadorai! Sir, I have just joined in the Info Systems department. I thought I should meet all the senior people and seek their blessings before I start,' said Gauri.

Ramadorai fell for the knighthood – he loved it when people called him 'sir'. He ordered coffee for Gauri and proceeded to ask if she was married (she wasn't) and all about her ancestors. After coffee, Gauri asked him how she should go about introducing computer support so that Sir would not have to work so hard.

She then started to show Ramadorai how he could very easily do the complicated accounting-related math using the computer. The old sod was unimpressed.

'I can do the mathematics much faster than this machine. My father used to make me do all the calculations in my head and I had to always be quicker than him or else I would get a sharp swipe of the cane. You should introduce this computer stuff to the other fellows who have not had the grounding in mathematics that most people in my generation have had. I notice the fellows from the north are not as good as us when it comes to mental stuff.'

Gauri wasn't about to give up. She said, 'That's a great idea, sir. I will work with you on converting the others. This will also provide you with a database of the employees. You can get any information about an employee at the press of a button. So if you wanted to look up any information about say, Mr Sanjay Mundra, Assistant Manager, Engineering Projects, you could get it at the press of a button.'

She then proceeded to show him how to navigate the screens and get to the information about Sanjay Mundra. I noticed that the old coot was not convinced. He rang the bell on his desk – a legacy of the colonial past. His old administrative assistant Jagrut Prasad peered in with a question mark stamped large on his face.

Ramadorai said, 'Prasad, tell me, when did Sanjay Mundra join the company?'

Jagrut said without a pause, 'Sir, exactly a month from now he will complete two years of service as Assistant Manager, Engineering Projects. Mr Mundra joined us on 14 March 1989. Before that he worked as a trainee for eighteen months.'

Ramadorai looked at Gauri and me victoriously and said, 'THAT is called information at the press of a button. Can the computer do that? No! So I don't need it cluttering up my table. If Jagrut needs it, give it to him.'

Gauri and I walked out of Ramadorai's room. Gauri was still upbeat. We had to get creative, she said.

I decided to drive down to the Taj and have dinner with Keya. It was Valentine's Day, after all. I called her office before I left Balwanpur. She was in a meeting, so I left a message that I was planning to stay at the hotel that night and that we should have dinner together. I had made a Valentine's Day card for her. I knew that she saved all the cards I sent her, just as I had a collection of her poems and observations, all put down on kite paper.

When I reached the hotel, the girl at the counter gave me my room key and an elaborately carved wooden case, not bigger than the size of my palm. She smiled as she saw the quizzical look on my face. I took the elevator to my room. I opened the door and almost jumped out of my skin. There was a bunch of balloons hanging from the ceiling and vases full of pink gladioli were strategically placed around the room. As I shut the door, Keya stepped out from behind the curtains and gave me a hug.

'Happy Valentine's Day, Abbey,' she said.

'Happy Valentine's Day, Keya. This also happens to be my sixth wedding anniversary, you know,' I said as I held her close and buried my nose in her hair.

'Your sixth wedding?'

'You know what I mean. Actually, I haven't had even one decent wedding. I wonder how Ayesha is celebrating this evening. Do you think she is with Kevin or has she moved on to someone with a bigger bank balance?'

Keya pointed to the balloons and said, 'Each one of them tells you why I love you. Don't you want to find out how I feel?'

She picked up the wooden box that I had been given at the reception and told me to open it. A tiny bottle of perfume nestled inside. The label said 'Amarige by Givenchy'. Just below the bottle was a needle. I looked at Keya quizzically. Then I took the needle and burst one of the balloons. A piece of paper fell out of it. It was the same kite paper on which Keya wrote love notes for me.

The note said, 'A thousand nights to solve the mysteries that have remained since you first held my soul – K.' The next balloon burst open to reveal a couplet by Mirza Ghalib. Having burst all the balloons in the room, I turned to Keya and said, 'One prick and it's gone. Just like my marriage with Ayesha.'

'Abbey, that relationship is dead and gone. Stop carrying the corpse around wherever you go.'

'Keya, why is that perfume called Amarige? Were they trying to spell marriage but got mixed up?'

Keya opened the bottle and smelt the perfume. 'Doesn't it smell good? The Japanese girl who sold it to me at the hotel told me that it had just been launched and that it needs to be applied to the pulse points on the body to be really effective.'

'Here, let me learn the art of putting perfume on a woman. Tell me where to start, Keya.'

'Inside the wrists... yeah... Abbey, you don't need to be so stingy... and now on this hand too... yeah... now put some behind the ears... stop biting, Abbey... the back of the neck... mmm...I like that... your warm breath on my neck... now on the temples... behind the knees... between my breasts... stop it, Abbey... between the toes... ankles... thighs...'

The next day was a Friday. We both decided to take off from work and spend it together. We just stayed in bed and talked. In the afternoon, we went for lunch to Tenzil's, a Tibetan restaurant that served the most delicious tofu with greens and corn soup. Keya insisted on using their Tibetan names – Tse Tofu and Ashom Tang.

From there we went to Connaught Place and then walked over to Janpath to buy junk jewellery for Keya. She couldn't get enough of it.

We were walking back with all the beads and stones when a young beggar stopped us to ask for money. Keya and I looked at the girl who must have been hardly fourteen or fifteen years old. She should have been in school, I thought. Keya grabbed the girl's hand and pulled her aside. She pulled out all the jewellery we had bought and gave it to the girl to try on. The girl was perplexed but elated.

Without any explanation, Keya took my hand and said, 'Let's go.'

The next morning, sitting in bed sipping coffee, Keya was back to her usual chirpy and upbeat self. She wanted to know why I was so pensive.

I didn't need any encouragement to vent. 'Why is my office full of these crazy people and problems? There must be an easier way to earn a living, Keya. Did I tell you about this fuck-up that I need to resolve? Our company needs to adopt computerization fast. I have been having a tough time trying to get our obtuse managers to take up new technology. If we do not computerize, we will never be able to survive in a highly computerized marketplace. If the managers don't get used to computers, how will we ever get the workers to adopt these tools?'

Keya sipped her coffee and doodled on the front page of the newspaper. Then she tossed her pen aside and looked at me.

'If your managers are resisting technology, maybe you should get the workers to adopt it. Why do you think the managers need to set an example in everything? If the workers resist it, get their kids to adopt new technology. By the way, Abbey, how many children can one legally adopt in a lifetime?'

'Keya, can we finish this discussion on adopting technology before we start talking about adopting kids? What's the point of getting the kids to adopt technology? We don't employ them.'

'All kids enjoy playing games. Get them used to playing with computers. Upload some simple games and invite them to play,' Keya suggested and then she changed the topic and said, 'Abbey, have you ever thought of spending a few months meditating in the mountains? It's supposed to be the best way to gain inner peace. I think that's what we should all do. Do I need to be a Buddhist to follow Buddha's style of meditation?'

I looked at Keya and marvelled at the gem of an idea she had proposed. I couldn't wait to get back to Balwanpur to try it out.

Five days later, the town was plastered with posters inviting children (and adults) to come and play games on the computers in the factory. Gauri had set up five computers in the temperature controlled rooms, all of which were decorated with posters of Disney characters. A few kids, accompanied by their parents, turned up rather hesitantly. Very soon, the parents were fighting with the children to have a go at the computers.

We organized a slogan contest. The winning slogan was 'Grow near with technology.' (Gronier with technology, get it?) Gauri and I would stand there watching the adults overcome their fear of technology. We knew that the battle had been won. A month later, we implemented the computerization project for the office staff. By the end of the year, the computers were a part of the officers' lives. Matt Keller was delighted. He called me to his office to discuss our plans for 1992.

By now I knew that Keller was a fanatic for presentations. Everything had to be put on slides with an accompanying Implementation Plan Calendar (or IPC, as it was known in Gronier's office lingo). He looked like the sort of person who went to bed in a starched shirt and tie with three slides and an IPC for his dreams.

Matt extended a firm handshake. He always started the conversation with one of three sentences: (a) Hi Abbey, how was the weekend? – if you met him on a Monday or Tuesday; (b) Hi Abbey, what are your plans for the coming weekend? – if you met him on a Thursday or Friday; (c) Hey Abbey, the weather is awful/awesome today, isn't it? – if it was a Wednesday.

This time he opened with option (a). I responded the

way I always did – with an enthusiastic 'It was fantastic, Matt. How was your weekend?' He responded as if he had just spent the weekend in bed with a porn star: 'TERRIFIC!'

This was one of the rituals Rusty had taught me to live with.

'When they ask you about your weekend, they are seeking to hear a one-word response and not a *War and Peace* version,' he had warned.

Matt ordered coffee as the next step of the ritual and then sat me down for a chat. His brief to me was clear. We needed to get 4000 of the 5000 workers off our payrolls.

'I am not sure if we can do that, Matt. There are legal issues and the union will not let us off that easily. It doesn't sound realistic. Why don't we think of absorbing the workers in some capacity? Gronier is a large corporation. There will be some opportunity that we can find…' I said as firmly as possible.

'The corporate office is clearly unhappy about us not making enough profits in the India operations. We need to trim our employee strength to remain globally competitive. Abbey, you have to be creative. I loved your idea of getting the children to play games on the computers so that the operators would be cajoled into taking up technology. If it had not been for your idea, I would not have implemented automation in the factory as step one of our Excess Staff Optimization Project (ESOP). You obviously have the foresight and strategic thinking to move two steps ahead. The workers must really trust you to have fallen for the video games bait!' Matt laughed hysterically.

'Matt, I didn't mean to use the games as bait. I did it because I genuinely believe that computerization is a skill everyone needs to have to be a part of this globalized world,' I said in a tone that betrayed my anger.

'The steps are clear. We have introduced computerization. That prepares the way for us to start introducing automation on the shopfloor so that our production numbers are not affected as we reduce the number of operators to about five hundred. Once the workers have gone, we can bring down the number of management staff to about fifty.'

I asked the rhetorical question: 'Matt, will I lose my job as well?'

'Yes. I'm afraid so. But it's nothing personal, you understand? You are a great guy, Abbey. I would love to have a drink with you any day and I think you are really smart, but we are running a business. And you are the only one who knows that you will be made redundant. That's because you have to carry out the downsizing project. You will be the last one to leave, though.'

'What if I take forever to complete this task?'

'You have six months' time to complete the lay-offs. You also have a headstart in trying to find yourself a job. So start calling up the headhunters. At this stage you don't need to tell them that you are being laid off. So there won't be any stigma attached to the transaction. You could spend the next thirty days trying to find a job.

Tell them that you will be ready to take up a new assignment from the first of January. Just get yourself a new job before it becomes public knowledge that Gronier is laying off its staff.'

'Matt, I've never done this before. I've given people jobs, never taken them away – unless it was over a disciplinary issue or when someone's integrity was in question. This is crazy. What if I choose to resign and not do this?'

'You would be a fool to do that. When your next employer calls me to do a reference check, do you want me to tell them that we had to let you go because you were not effective enough?'

'You can't do that. You won't be able to carry out the lay-offs. Your plan will fail.' I tried to think on my feet.

'Don't fuck with me, Abbey. Gronier will just shut down the India operations. I will move on to my new assignment to another country. You will be responsible for ruining the lives of innocent people and their families. On the other hand, if you design a Voluntary Retirement Scheme or VRS as they say, the employees will get enough money to live with dignity until they find their next job. You have a responsibility towards the employees. Your choice will impact their fate.'

'Are you trying to emotionally blackmail me?'

'Heck no!' Matt switched on the charm then and said, 'I am asking for your help. We could either shut down the factory and throw all five thousand people out of a job or we could try and buy some time for ourselves. Maybe we could keep a thousand people on the rolls and try to leverage the automation you have introduced in the factory to compete in the global marketplace. I kind of thought that given your long association with the factory, you would try and keep at least a thousand people on board.'

I left his office very confused. The prospect of keeping one thousand people on the rolls was marred by the thought of getting rid of four thousand. I felt numb. It was still to sink in that I was going to be made redundant.

I thought of the organizational behaviour classes at MIJ. Some research done on cancer patients had showed that when they first learnt about the disease, they went through shock, anger, resignation and finally acceptance – the SARA model. I was clearly in stage one of SARA – in deep shock.

*How the fuck can the company do this to me? I've done such a great job over the last few years. Doesn't that have any meaning? I feel like a rag that has been used to wipe the dirt and then discarded in the garbage dump. I am a piece of garbage. I've lost my job. Fuck Gronier and Matt Kaller. May he rot in hell. Dirty sonovabitch.*

*He has given you extra time to look for a job. So he must really like you.*

*Of course he does. That's why he started the process by appointing me as the chosen one who would lay off thousands of people.*

I went back to my apartment and sat on the chair near the window in my bedroom. The sky was grey and looking at it depressed me even further. It was a strange feeling, to be in HR and worrying about not having a job. I had always been the one who gave people jobs and shook them by the hand after handing them their appointment letter. But here I was, thinking of Matt Keller and what a heartless dog he was to have just sacked me – albeit with six months' notice. The bastard gave me a generous six months' notice not because he cared for me and wanted to give me time to find a job, but because the task he had assigned to me would need that kind of time. He was counting on my credibility with the workers to pull it off. Anyone else would take longer or cause a major labour problem. I had always known the world was full of Matt Kellers. But this was the first time I was meeting one at such close quarters.

I had to find myself a job before I went on a sacking spree. For some strange reason, I thought of Pinaki Rahan, my Bengali friend from school, and what he had said to me a long time ago:

'Bradaar, remembaar always, life is a beach.'

I would immediately step in to correct him. 'You mean to say, life is a bitch?'

'Yessss! That is what I said. Life is a beach.'

## TWENTY-THREE

Rascal Rusty had told me that the first big rule of looking for a job was to never approach the placement consultant. That shows you are desperate. You have to wait for the phone to ring. But I had no time. I had to break the rules.

I called Bob D'Souza, a partner in India's biggest placement firm, KLPD Consultants. The firm's name represented the initials of the four founding members: Khanna, Lohia, Panigrahi and D'Souza. They had all made their millions by placing people in jobs and charging the firm thirty-three per cent of the sucker's pay package. The bigger the salary negotiated with the firm, the bigger the commission KLPD would make. What a great business model to work with, especially when somebody else did all the pleading and crawling to negotiate a better fee. Over the years, Khanna left to marry a girl from Italy and set up a bakery in Milan, Lohia went back to Kanpur to join his family business, and Panigrahi died of cirrhosis of the liver, brought about by excessive Walking, I was told. (He was a Johnny Walker addict!)

D'Souza was known for his preference for young boys and his rather feminine style of speaking. Right now, he was the face of hope for me.

'Hey Abbey! How nice of you to call. I thought you guys didn't believe in working with KLPD. We are not like the typical placement firm, you know, whose job is to coax a resume out of the candidate and forward it to you. We are a boutique search firm. We are in the business of matchmaking.'

'Hi Bob! Actually, this is for myself. I am looking for a change. I have been with Balwanpur for almost eight years now. It's time to look for something different.'

'Is something wrong? Why would you want to leave such a good life? I have never known a man who wants to quit being a frog in that well. Tell me the real story, Abbey.'

*This bastard is sharp. Maybe he knows that I have been sacked. If he does, I am dead. Maybe I need to talk to someone more reliable. Or approach a company directly.*

I made a list of companies and located their address and telephone numbers with considerable effort. I would go to the shops and look for the company's address on the product labels. That's how I got the addresses of those who made Iodex, Nescafe, Colgate. It took me a long time to type out my resume. I thought of the advice Rusty had given me when I first made my resume as a student in MIJ. He had explained to me the difference between a resume, a bio-data and a CV (Curriculum Vitae). Rusty knew everything about everything. But right now, I needed a job. Time was running out.

I was getting obsessed. I started to look for addresses of companies every time I went to buy something from a store. From hair oil to watches, I took down addresses and mailed a copy of my resume. Several companies had to be eliminated from the list because I knew that someone from MIJ was already working there. I couldn't let my classmates know that I was looking for a job. An MBA never looks for a job – jobs always seek out him or her. Why was this not happening to me? What was I doing wrong?

I wondered if I should call Rusty. He was not in India and he didn't have too many friends at MIJ.

*That won't work. He has been in touch with Ayesha. Isn't it logical that he would tell Ayesha? She is your wife, after all. Maybe she could even do something about it.*

*Like what? Ask Kevin to loan me some money? Stop being daft.*

*She might know people here who would be able to help. Her dad knows influential people.*

*Over my dead body. I'll starve but I'll never ask them for anything.*

*I wish I could share this with my parents, but they would go into deep shock. Ma would worry about it endlessly.*

*Maybe if you shared your agony with someone, it would help. Share it with Keya.*

*No, she wouldn't understand.*

*Ayesha?*

*She doesn't care. I haven't been in touch with her since she left and I can't suddenly invite her to go job hunting with me.*

The newspapers had been picking up titbits of information about Gronier Inc., US being unhappy about the high cost of operating the factory at Balwanpur and how that was impacting its share value on Wall Street. The newspapers should be banned from writing shit that makes it difficult for someone to find a job. The headhunters all seemed to have an inkling that all was not well. It's funny how power equations change. When they were calling me, I had the upper hand. They would keep following up and ask if there was any business I could offer. Now that I was calling them for a job, suddenly they were all too busy to take my call. Even if they did, they were completely insensitive to the urgency of the matter.

One of the sods even said, 'This week, I am busy with a golf tournament. I've promised myself I won't look at a single resume until I've improved my handicap.'

I made a mental note to kick his ass big time as soon as I got a decent job. Didn't the bastard realize that his focus on golf was taking away precious time? I swore to myself that I would always remain sensitive to others' timelines and sense of urgency. Maybe this was God's way of punishing me for keeping some job applicant waiting. How I hated being at the receiving end of the power equation!

Meanwhile, I had to start work on the VRS schemes. I

drove back to Balwanpur, thinking of the challenge ahead of me. It was probably the most difficult journey I had ever made. I felt like someone sneaking home in the darkness of the night, murder weapon concealed but ready for the kill. Was I doing the right thing?

*You are a professional who is paid to keep the organization competitive. This is no time to be sentimental.*

*I am also human, damn it. I can't do something clinically because it keeps my employer competitive. I also have some accountability towards the employees. What about their feelings? What about mine? It's not just about doing your job.*

*You don't have a job any more. You HAD one. Executing the VRS to perfection is your job now.*

I had not realized that I was actually rather fond of the people in the factory. They were my own. I could sit down and find a million faults in everything that they did, yet, if an outsider said anything about them, I would take up arms to defend them. The town had a special place in my heart. This was where I started my career. This was where I got my first promotion. Ayesha and I set up our home here for the first time. But now I had been entrusted with the task of destroying the very fabric of the place.

Half an hour after I had checked into the managers' guesthouse, my phone started to ring. Mrs Dayal was calling to say she expected me home for dinner.

Time was of the essence. I started to craft some alternative proposals that I could sell to the board as being financially viable, yet fair to the employees. I wondered how Father Hathaway would react to my dilemma. The Scottish priest had always taught us to do the right thing. He used to say, 'nihil ultra' – nothing is beyond.

I finally had to talk to Baba and explain to him that I had to go about designing a separation scheme and that it was hurting my conscience to put so many people out of a job. Despite myself, I ended up telling him that at the end of the assignment I would also be out of a job. Baba was surprisingly calm about it. I begged him not to share the news with Ma and Asmita. He promised.

Baba said, 'Chotka, you are here on this earth to carry out a task that God wants you to do. He has equipped you to do it by making you an HR professional. You have to do the task as best as you can. Lord Krishna told Arjuna on the battlefield  that he could only do his task. The consequences were not for him to worry about.'

'Baba, isn't that a rather fatalistic attitude towards life?'

'On the contrary, the *Bhagwad Gita* tells you not to lose focus by letting the possible outcome distract you from the task. If we all did our task with hundred per cent dedication, the result would be exactly what the task was designed to achieve. If you do not have a job, remember we are always here for you. Just come back home.'

I had to decide who to coopt as a partner in the project. It had to be someone who was savvy with numbers.  Maybe

I should get Ramadorai to create the proposal. That would also help to seed the idea among the other employees. For nothing that the accounts department of the factory knew remained a secret for long. Besides, Ramadorai would make sure that it was a numerically sound, foolproof proposal. 'Keep your friends close and your enemies closer,' I thought.

Ramadorai always brought out the cruel streak in me. Now I would get him to work with me to prepare the proposal and then offer the first VRS to him. That would be sweet revenge. All these years Ramadorai had pulled out the rule book to set up a roadblock for any proposal I designed. He had obviously not forgiven me for having denied him the opportunity to be my father-in-law. Now I would make the old coot tie the knot that he would use to hang himself.

Ramadorai first wanted to know if the scheme would be directed at newcomers (presumably me) or people with seniority of service (like him) or anyone who wanted to take the money and go. I was smart. I told him to work out options that would apply to all three categories. He did an amazing job, I must say. He did a detailed analysis of all the employees, based on their length of service, and worked out two plans – one for the workers and one for the officers and managers. He worked out the cost impact of both schemes and the numbers looked good. All I had to do was get a sign-off from Matt and I was ready to start with the first of the layoffs.

On D-day I called Ramadorai to my office. He did not suspect anything. He came with a bunch of calculations and his calculator. Here was my chance to get back at him for all those times that he threw the rulebook at me. Here was sweet revenge. I cleared my throat.

'Mr Ramadorai, no one knows the details of the VRS better than you. I am sorry, but it is my job to offer this scheme to you first. Nothing personal... I do hope...'

'What? Are you trying to act funny with me, young man? I will file a written complaint against you if you do not apologize immediately for this silly prank.'

'No, Mr Ramadorai... this is for real. You know that the company can afford to keep only a thousand workers and a hundred officers. So I am afraid there is no choice. You are one of the managers to whom we must first offer the option of taking this rather attractive Voluntary Retirement Scheme.'

Then Ramadorai did something unexpected. He grabbed my hand and broke down in tears.

'How can the company do this to me after all the years of loyal service I have rendered? When my wife died, I came back to the office from the burning ghat because it was the annual accounts closing time. So this is my reward? Tell me... this is my reward for loyal work. Correct?' He was almost shouting. I offered him a glass of water.

'God cannot be so cruel. I have responsibilities. You know, when my wife died, I had to look after my daughter and manage my own life here in the office. It was tough to take care of a little child who did not understand why she didn't have a mother like all the other children. My little girl used to stay up past midnight until I went home after the accounts work was done. She was so scared to be home alone. Yet, I did not ever let my personal problems come in the way of my professional duties. The company must give me some credit for those years. You can't just throw me out. At least, not until Rajani is married. Please understand my situation... please... If Lord Murugesan is going to test me, then all I want to say is that I have no more strength left to fight. I am an old man. I can't... I just can't...'

Ramadorai was no longer the enemy I had to seek revenge against. This was not the N.S.R. Ramadorai who was called 'No Sorry Regret Ramadorai' because of his ability to point out a rule that would enable him to deny you the simple joys of life. All I saw was a tired old man wiping his tears and shaking his head in disbelief, and trying to keep his dignity intact. I walked across from my desk and sat in the chair next to him and just held his hand. After a long silence, he seemed to accept the situation and asked me where he should sign. He took the sheaf of papers and walked home. Even as he left, I could see him shaking his head at the unfairness of it all.

I knew it would not be long before I did the same. I was feeling quite sick. I went home early. I poured out a large shot of Old Monk and sipped it. It tasted bitter. I had forgotten to add Thums Up. I sat in silence and wondered what Ramadorai would do. Had he shared the news with Rajani? The answer came soon enough. My phone rang. It was Rajani on the phone. She was sobbing and was quite incoherent.

'You bastard. You creep. You are going to kill Appa. He is just lying on the bed and staring at the ceiling. He is in deep shock. He calls out my mother's name and cries. What has he done to harm you, you crazy bastard? If he dies of shock, will you achieve an even better rating at your appraisal?'

'Rajani, I am sorry… I had to do this. He is not the only one… the company has to remain competitive and so we have to trim down to the bare minimum… Maybe this is just the right time for your dad to start some financial consultancy work on his own…'

'Oh, stop being such a do-gooder! And thanks for your concern after you have destroyed my father. He had only two years left for retirement. It's strange to imagine that he was stopping Gronier from becoming globally competitive. Wow! That's a new one. You bastard… I hope you rot in hell.' She was hysterical.

I hung up. The news of the VRS spread like wildfire in the township. It was all that people spoke of all the time. Over the next few months, I had all kinds of ugly epithets slung at me. Why didn't these buggers understand that I too felt like a hangman every time I called someone to my office? They all knew that it was the kiss of death. It was a horrible feeling to be hated by everyone around me. Conversations would stop as soon as I walked into a room. I stopped going out altogether – partly because no one invited me home anyway. It got particularly ugly when I had to call Mrs Dayal to offer her the VRS. She fainted in the office. We had to get the ambulance from our dispensary to rush her to the Intensive Care Unit. She suffered a stroke that left her right side paralysed. I didn't know what to do. The only way to cope was to completely shut off any feelings and work on auto-mode. I repeatedly told myself that it was only a bloody job that I was doing. There was nothing personal about it. Yet, it was not easy. Nothing was easy, not even falling asleep at the end of a hard day. I lost weight. I had no appetite for all the good food that the cook at the guest house prepared. Maybe it was age catching up... The mid-thirties is a dangerous age, I reflected.

One day, I came back home and sat down on the sofa with a glass of OM2. I had to take stock. What would be the next logical step for Matt? There was only one person who could answer the question.

'Hey Rusty, bad news. A Voluntary Retirement Scheme is being offered at our factory. It will knock off almost four hundred of the office staff. It's pretty crazy.'

'That, my friend, is a great oxymoron – Voluntary Retirement. Companies should formally rename it as CRS, given that most times, it's compulsory and not voluntary. When you eat an egg, that's called a voluntary act. It is not a voluntary act when you have to eat tandoori chicken.' Rusty laughed at his own joke.

'Rusty, what do you think they will do next? Maybe after this they will ask me to go as well. You'd better find me a decent job.' I had to find an innocuous way to ask him for a job.

'They can't do that. This is your time to bargain, Abbey. Don't let the opportunity go. The next logical step is going to be factory automation. They will announce a VRS for workers as well. This is the time when your CEO needs you the most. He won't be able to navigate the labour laws without your help. Your credibility with the workers is already high. Ask and you shall receive. This is the time to ask for a promotion. Go for the kill, Abbey.'

I thought of telling him that I needed a job, but decided against it. 'Rusty, my conscience is hurting. The officers' VRS scheme gave them a pittance. They will not be able to live with dignity on such a meagre sum. I have killed so many of my friends – even their families have not been spared.'

Rusty did not respond to my pain. He said casually, 'Hey, I met Ayesha last week in Manhattan. Her boutique looks great. I told her that you are now a vice president and have it all. She really misses you. Listen, I have a charity dinner to attend with Amitabh Bachchan, yeah, the film star. He is in Dubai on a private visit. Bye.'

I called someone I had not spoken to for a long time. The guy who would know what to do. I called Captain Sobti.

'Hi Abbey! So what makes you think of Captain Sobti? You are a vice president – the president of all vices!' He laughed like a man possessed.

'Captain, I need your counsel. The company needs only a thousand people in phase one. Once we become competitive in the global market, we will be able to take back the other four thousand.'

'Don't give me that shit, Abbey. Do you seriously believe that the company will take back four thousand workers after getting rid of them? Next you will tell me that Santa Claus has promised to deliver these jobs. I like your sense of humour, Abbey. Let's cut to the chase, shall we? The simple solution is that you call Negi and tell him that you will pay him a hundred rupees for every person he persuades to accept the VRS package. He will do the needful. He will hire goons to cause industrial unrest, then shut down the factory. A month later he will float a rumour that the factory is being shut permanently. A month later, when the workers are desperate, you can implement a low-cost VRS. As soon as four thousand people have signed up, start the factory with the thousand people left on the rolls. The workers will sign whatever he tells them to. He is known to have killed people before.'

'Like the time he tried to kill you for raping his wife?' I wanted to say but did not.

I could hear voices in the background as we spoke. The clink of glasses, a giggle, the faint sound of music. I was clearly interrupting. Five thousand – or perhaps one thousand – jobs were at stake. I hung up. I had to do this myself.

I needed to take the union into confidence. I would have to talk to all the workers and address their fears.

If I was scared, I couldn't blame them for being terrified. I needed an ally and it could not be Negi. Arai was the one who had the trust of the workers. I spoke to him about my dilemma and told him about the VRS. He was shocked. He said he needed a day to think it over. He came back the same evening and told me that he would work with me, but in turn I had to give him my word that I would be fair to the workers. The officers' VRS had left a lot of people with a sense of impending doom. He kept asking me if there was a way out by which we could avoid doing this to the workers. I told him that all the options had been explored and rejected. Finally, we decided to talk to all five thousand workers in small groups. Arai suggested that we invite the families to the discussion.

'How will we manage to feed our families? We need the job. The money is only a short-term solution,' said Nirmal, the electrician I had displaced at the barber's shop.

Arai thundered, 'You do not need a job. You need to earn a living and for that you need skills that are employable. The place where you earn a living could be different. What matters is whether you are employable or not.'

With each group, the conversation was the same. 'I will try to tie up with an institute that will train you in various vocational skills over the next two weeks. They also provide placements to most students, but the job may be in another company and probably in another city.

Meanwhile, you will need to invest the money that you get from the VRS so that it can last you for the next couple of years. I will ask Mr N.S.R. Ramadorai to come and teach people about investment options. He has started a firm that has helped so many of our officers. I will arrange to pick up the cost of his consulting fees. If you play it right, this could well be an opportunity.'

That night I sat back and tried to rethink the approach. What I needed to do was shape the board's perspective on its relationship with India. I would have to get Matt Keller and his peers to understand that it was in their best interests to take a long-term view of India. The company needed to be seen as an MNC with a difference. A company that prioritized shareholder value creation but was also concerned about making a contribution to the local community and the nation. This approach would stand it in good stead since India was potentially a big market, perhaps one of the most attractive markets of the future, if Rascal Rusty was to be believed. Therefore, while making operations productive was important, the company must think in terms of making a contribution to the township of Balwanpur. We would need to create livelihoods and sustain the economy of the town and the surrounding areas, rather than allow it to collapse with the redundancy package.

I put together a proposal for a livestock upgradation programme followed by a milk marketing initiative. Even the poorest households owned two or three heads of cattle. If, through a programme of artificial insemination, livestock could be upgraded, milk yields could increase three-fold and create a huge economic opportunity for the township. In fact, it would be possible to involve all five thousand workers' households in the initiative and the income would match the money they were used to making.

In addition, my proposal recommended that Gronier invest in promoting a milk marketing initiative. Four milk-chilling plants would have to be set up across the district, with a nominal capital investment. This would provide the infrastructure to collect and market milk, to generate significant economic activity in the township.

If this was done, Gronier would be seen to be giving back to the local community and making a solid contribution to the social sector. And it would be much easier to implement the proposed restructuring. An alternative income stream would in the process be created for those workmen who would have to be separated. I spent four days locked up in a room trying to put together a ten-slide presentation on the project.

Sophie used to say, 'A presentation is a story that you tell an audience. It must be the answer to a question. So before you start making the presentation, ask yourself what is the key question you are trying to answer.'

The milk marketing plan was the answer to the question 'What can the Gronier Corporation do to minimize the negative perceptions in the media arising out of the massive lay-offs?' Instead of hiring a PR firm to put out fires, my proposal suggested a proactive way of building Gronier's reputation as an employer with a conscience.

Rascal Rusty would have said, 'People only chase their self-interest. Any benefit you have derived is only incidental and not intended.' But Rusty was a cynic. Whether it was Sophie's style of presentation or Rusty's belief that the board acted in its own self-interest and the residents of Balwanpur were incidental beneficiaries, my proposal for the rehabilitation of workers was approved.

With that approval in my pocket, I presented the second part of my plan – to rehabilitate the management staff impacted by the lay-offs.

'Step one is to communicate to the management staff that if the company is to grow, the operations have to become more productive,' I said. 'Though some of them would need to separate, we could provide them with an opportunity to participate in the future prosperity of the company through an employee stock option plan.'

I went on to explain the technicalities of how to make that work. I told them the board would need the approval of the shareholders to enhance equity by three per cent as this would be the additional equity required to implement such a scheme. By increasing equity by three per cent, equity dilution for the parent company would be one per cent and it would not therefore be a major issue to contend with. The scheme would build confidence and enhance our own credibility among the management staff. We could also give the affected employees four months' time to rehabilitate themselves in other companies.

Matt Keller seemed to be the greatest supporter of the plan. He surprised me by defending the proposal and finally, to my delight, the board approved a plan that would enable me to look the workers and the officers in the eye and still carry out the redundancy plan. This time, the drive back to Balwanpur did not seem as grim and unbearable.

I went to meet Arai at his home. Arai loved the idea of the milk cooperative. We joined hands to communicate in a systematic manner to the workmen the inevitability of the restructuring process. We had to convince them with facts and figures that it was untenable to carry on the way we were.

Arai explained the scheme to groups of workmen and their families. Workmen with less than five years' service left would be given their salary for the next two years, so that they were in a position to rehabilitate. This would take care of a thousand workmen. The company would offer a voluntary separation scheme with compensation based on past years of service to another three thousand workmen over the next four months.

Sometimes I wished I had four months to look for a job for myself. Even though Matt had given me six months' notice, I had not been able to do anything about it.

Finally, there came the day when I could call Matt and assure him that all four thousand people would be off our rolls by November.

'Will any of these workers try any litigation against us?' Matt asked.

'Matt, the short answer to that question is no. Once they sign a Voluntary Retirement Scheme and accept the money, they have given up their right to litigate against the company,' I replied.

'If you can assure me of zero litigation, I could sweeten the deal even more with money from some discretionary funds that I have. In exchange for a waiver of all rights to take the matter to court, I will pay for the cost of vocational training to each worker for six months at the local Technical Training Institute. That should help them find jobs.'

'One last thing, Matt...'

'Yes?'

'Make these changes effective as of last June. That will ensure that every one of the employees who has been laid off has a shot at rebuilding his or her life.' I swear I thought of Ramadorai's face as I said this.

In the end, what each of the workers got was a better than industry average on the VRS proposal, thanks to the extra money Matt threw in. Some of the younger workers found jobs in the ancillary industries that operated in the vicinity of the township. The Technical Training Institute had a placement cell that provided jobs to about fifteen hundred workers with the K.K. Shah group that was setting up a plant in a nearby state.

The whole exercise left me feeling emotionally drained. I came back to my apartment in Delhi and decided that now that I had done the right thing by the workers and managers, it was time to find myself a job.

I had not noticed Keya's presence. She leaned against the main door and paused for a long time before speaking. She was looking at me as if she was observing an animal in the zoo.

'What are you feeling right now? Are you more worried about being hated by all the officers and workers of the Balwanpur township, or are you afraid of losing your job? Or are you anxious about what it will look like on your resume, being on the rolls of a company that is knocking off people?' Keya was really asking the right questions.

I responded as best as I could. 'All of the above, I think. The fear of being out of a job is very real. I have never come so close to being unemployed. We all joke about wanting to retire early, but when it comes to the crunch, it's a scary thought. I am scared of losing it all. I am scared of losing you. All these years, I took things for granted. But now...'

Keya held out a small book to me and said, 'A Zen Master was once summoned by the king of the land. The king bowed to the monk and asked him what egotism meant. The Master admonished the king and said it was a stupid question that did not befit a man of his stature. The king was angry and upset and looked it. The Master said gently, "This is egotism." I believe, Abbey, that we are all trying continuously to change the direction of the river in which we are sailing. But the river will not change its course. You can only row your boat through your own actions. Life will go on – flow with it, my friend.'

'Where did you learn all this, Keya? You sound like a Zen Master.' The day had left me exhausted. I stifled a yawn.

The phone rang. It was Gopher. It took me a minute to make the connection, for the operator had said that Mr Gopuram Ramesh, of K.K. Shah group, wanted to speak to me.

'Hi Abbey! This is Ramesh. I need a favour.'

'Hi Gopher! What can I do you for you?'

'I'll make this quick. We are looking for someone to head Human Resources for our group. You are the best person I can think of. You have worked in the same industry and now that we have taken so many workers from Gronier's factory, your connect with them would be invaluable. The money would be good too.'

'Why aren't you taking the job?' I could never trust Gopher. There had to be a catch.

'I got a break with these guys and moved to the marketing department. It was something I had always wanted to do. I believe I am better at managing brands than people. You are much better at that. Don't say no, you crazy bugger. At least meet our new managing director, Vivek Shah. Vicky did his MBA from the US and has just returned to India to take over the business from his father. He is very different and wants to change the nature of the family business by working with the best professionals.'

Gopher spent half an hour trying to persuade me. But I couldn't bring myself to take charity from someone I had always hated.

*Isn't it amazing that Gopher, who knows how much I dislike him, is actually the first to offer me a job? It shows how wrong one can be about people.*

*People change. But in your mind, you did not allow room for Gopher to grow.*

I woke up to the sound of Raga Ahir Bhairav, the legendary voice of Ustad Amir Khan rendering the morning raga as a variant of the original Raga Bhairav. I looked at my watch. It was four in the morning. I could visualize the scene in the living room. Keya would be sitting by the window, waiting for the first glimpse of dawn. The window would be open and the white lace curtains would be swaying in the cool breeze to the accompaniment of the wind chimes hanging in the corner. They sounded like the cowbells used by the Ahirs, which was what had supposedly inspired the creation of the raga, according to Keya. Ahir Bhairav, she told me, keeps the musical framework of Raga Bhairav but adds a few notes that are reminiscent of cowbells.

I rolled over and went back to sleep. The pillow still smelt of her. When my eyes opened again, it was ten o'clock. It was a Sunday, so there was no cause for panic. I called out to Keya but got no response. I got out of bed and went looking for her. There was a bunch of papers and a pen on the table in the living room. I went to the bathroom to check if she had left a poem for me on the mirror. Nothing.

I walked back to the living room and picked up the paper on top.

7 November 1992, 4:00 a.m.
Written to the Raga Ahir Bhairav

Yesterday was a very important day in my life.
My worst fears came true. My manager decided to
promote me to a bigger job. Despite my telling
him over and over again that I did not want to be
rewarded by anyone, he still gave me a promotion.
To not promote someone who has done a good job
is against the company's policy. Not respecting
my wishes is not. Strange!

When I met you at MIJ I felt that you were a
brave person, Abbey. You seemed so secure and
contented. You looked like a person who had learnt
to play with the universe. A person who had learnt
to ride the wave of time and did not need a safety
net.

Yesterday when I saw how scared you were of
losing your job, I saw how important power and
position have become for you. Instead of setting
you free, losing your job has only shackled you
further to the workplace.

It was you who taught me to stand up to my
own fears and anxieties. Now, more than ever, I
realize that there is so much I have to learn in this
lifetime. I am leaving, Abbey. I am going to
discover the Buddha in me. Most of all, I have to
learn to live without you and discover how to live
as my own person. To be free from all fears,

attachments and insecurities is the best way to discover one's soul. I do not even understand myself, Abbey. How will I ever understand you?

I am going to travel across India to find a master who can help me in my search for myself. Please respect my wishes and do not look for me. I will be back when our souls are ready for each other. You will always remain an integral part of my being.

All my love forever

Keya

I ran out to look for Keya, though I knew that it was futile. She would be on a bus to some unknown destination. I thought of all the places she had mentioned in the recent past, but the list was too long. I would just have to wait patiently for her to contact me. I briefly toyed with idea of lodging a missing-person complaint with the police and then thought better of it.

I asked myself what I could possibly have done to get Keya to stay and discover the Buddha within the confines of my apartment. I couldn't come up with a single idea.

# TWENTY-FOUR

$F$ather Hathaway was planning to be in Delhi during the first weekend of November. It was his annual trip to meet the mandarins at the ministry. I had booked a room for him at the guesthouse of the Gronier Corporation in CP and planned to meet him for dinner. I was really looking forward to catching up with Haathi.

The Scottish priest was one of seven priests who had come to India in 1945 with a common dream. Two years later, MIJ was started in a small room of Hotel Bistupur in Jamshedpur. The first batch of six students who graduated from MIJ were employed as personnel officers with the Steel and Iron Company. Over the years, Father Hathaway riding his Royal Enfield down the Bistupur market had become a sight familiar to everyone in the town.

Haathi shuffled into the dining hall of the guesthouse, talking to the peons and the waiters. He looked older than I had expected him to. He gave me a big hug and told me that the last time he had seen me my eyes had been closed, but he was used to seeing me that way in class anyway.

'Father, it's so nice to see you. Let's grab a plate each and then we can chat.' I walked with him to the buffet and noticed that he only took some salad.

'How do you look back on the last eight years of work in the corporate sector? You are one of our success stories. What are you at Gronier Corporation? You must be a senior manager now,' said Haathi.

I handed my business card to Haathi and said, 'Er... actually I am... umm... now called Vice President, Human Resources of Gronier Corporation, India.'

We settled down at a table with our plates and started to eat. After a short, not uncomfortable silence, I looked up and said, 'The big question is, what do I do next? Yes, I am now the head of Human Resources, a position I have always dreamt of getting and I got it sooner than I thought. Yet, it feels really hollow. Maybe it's a case of "I do not value what I get and I do not get what I value." I sometimes feel depressed that I have nothing more to look forward to... you know... like a big project which will allow me to make a difference to the world, and myself.' I was telling him more than I had planned to.

'Hmm... you haven't changed, I can see. Most executives need to have a coach to talk them through these dilemmas. Even in the case of a spiritual quest, the questions keep gnawing at you till you finally get down on your knees and talk to God and ask Him for an answer.

To find out if something has been worth it, you have to judge it by what you have given up rather than by what you have got. What we mean by success is something we have to ask ourselves before we start the journey. With people reaching the top in their thirties, the big challenge for the corporations will be to deal with boredom.' As usual, Haathi could go from the sublime to the mundane in the space of five lines.

'I can't say that I have not enjoyed the success – the power, the perks and the ability to shape an organization through one's work. But you're always under a microscope. Somebody is watching you and waiting for you to make a mistake so they can take it all away. The price I have paid has been on the personal front. I have not had enough time with the people who matter – my parents, my sister and so many others. You know that Ayesha and I are separated,' I confided.

'I know about that. Whatever happens is for the best. God has his ways of teaching us lessons that we need to learn and creating opportunities for us till we have mastered those lessons.' Father Hathaway had heard confessions before and knew how to be non-judgmental about people.

He continued, 'The hardest thing for executives is to face the changing nature of relationships. From relationships that are built on love and trust, you slowly discover that the world now is full of people who relate to you on the basis of what they can get from you. Barter becomes the basis of every relationship. And that's not easy for anyone to get used to. You need to learn to reach out and also look back and connect with your classmates. They are all senior managers. Talk to them about your dilemmas, they might have the solutions. Don't let your ego come in the way. In fact, we're planning an alumni meet for your batch over the Christmas weekend. Make sure you come. ' Haathi looked straight into my eyes as he spoke. It was almost as though he knew how hungry I was for a job.

So I told him the whole truth. That I was without a job and that I badly needed to find one before the end of the year.

'Organizations expect unwavering loyalty from their employees but when they have to choose between their interests and the interests of their employees, they always ignore the employees. Does the organization ever think of the devastation a lay-off can cause in the life of a human being?' I couldn't conceal my hurt.

Father Hathway was thoughtful. 'In India, the employer employs the entire family of the individual. The family's identity is impacted by the organization. So when they ask an employee to leave, they take away the sense of pride of the parents, the spouse, the children... that's very cruel. The emotional impact of the lay-off is so much more than just the loss of livelihood. Work gives meaning to life. If most of your identity resides in the business card in your wallet, then the moment the organization shreds that card, the individual's identity also gets dismantled. So never let an organization determine who you are. I am saying this to you Abbey, but I also realize my own identity is deeply intertwined with that of MIJ. If someone took that away, I would probably lose my sense of purpose in life.'

He spoke slowly and deliberately. 'Abbey, I once read a book by Viktor Frankl called *Man's Search for Meaning*. The story is about Frankl's experiences in a Nazi camp. He writes about the three stages every person went through: the initial shock that they experienced when they first entered, which was replaced with apathy once they got used to life in the camp, and finally the third reaction, of bitterness and disillusionment. According to Frankl, if you can't change a situation, it means that life is challenging you to change yourself.'

'Why am I going through this suffering, Father? I have lost all my self-respect and my dignity.' I could feel the sting of tears behind my eyelids.

'Look at it this way, Abbey. You are experiencing the meaning of life through this suffering. It's a valuable opportunity that life has given you.'

Haathi was like an old uncle with whom I could be myself. I didn't have to wear the mask of a person who is always in charge. Just being with him was a calming experience, and I loved every moment of our meeting. I would have answered every uncomfortable question, had he asked – even if it was about Ayesha. Only, he did not broach the subject.

I came back to my apartment after dropping Father off at the Jesuit Residence in Old Delhi where he was staying with friends. The next day I booked my ticket to Jamshedpur. A few weeks later I was boarding Tatanagar Express to go back to Jamshedpur – to retrace my memories, and to ask my classmates for a job.

The journey was painful. I thought of the pretence I would have to keep up on campus. Every institute expects their alumni to be successful and because of the pressure to conform, people in situations like mine end up feeling even smaller. Has anyone ever said this to the people who organize alumni reunions? Do we ever stop to ask ourselves the real reason why some of our classmates never turn up for alumni dinners? While comparing visiting cards, do we even stop to wonder why a friend 'forgot to carry business cards'? I knew how I felt going back to MIJ as a failure and not as the success story that everyone thought we would all be.

I tossed and turned all night, unable to sleep. I wondered if people would laugh at me behind my back. Would they pity me? I stared out of the window and watched the inky sky turn pale to signal the arrival of dawn.

This was the time for Ahir Bhairav.

*O great connoisseur of music, please focus on the fact that you are a failure. At alumni reunions, the alumni compare the number of promotions each one has got and how much faster one's career has moved compared to the peer group. You have redefined the race. You will be the first person to return to MIJ as an unemployed bum. Shame on you.*

Luckily for me, I didn't meet anyone on the way to MIJ. I even managed to reach the Executive Development Centre and check in without having met a single classmate.

*Isn't it strange that you are here to beg before your classmates and friends to give you a job and you are not doing anything to ensure that you succeed in that mission? You can't afford to have an ego, Abbey. What was that about beggars and choosers...*

Much as I wanted to, I couldn't shut off the voice in my head.

## TWENTY-FIVE

Cauvita and I have been sitting on the steps of the MIJ auditorium for a while. My mind is on Keya. Once, every rain-soaked afternoon used to be spent in the green room of this very auditorium. It was here that we discovered our bodies and left behind our innocence. She would emerge from her class and walk towards the auditorium, avoiding the curious gaze of MIJ-ites like Gopher who had nothing better to do than live vicariously.

My cigarette has long since burnt itself out. In a little while I will have to go across and join the bunch of corporate jetsetters and ask them for help. I want to delay the moment of humiliation as long as I can.

Cauvita nudges me and I become conscious that I have not answered her question. 'So which company did you join after leaving MIJ?'

Before I can answer her, I see 'Pocket Bahadur' running towards me, waving frantically. On reflex, I move a few inches away from Cauvita.

The Gurkha security guards at MIJ are part of its history. As far as I know, they have always been referred to by the generic term 'Bahadur' by the students. Only 'Pocket Bahadur' has a separate moniker because of his short stature. He is panting as he pulls himself to his full height of 4' 8" and tells me that there is an 'urgent' phone call for me. My mother is looking for me.

My heart sinks. I wonder if Baba and Ma are all right. I run towards the MIJ office, only to learn that the caller has promised to ring back in ten minutes. The ten longest minutes of my life.

Cauvita has followed me into the office. She gives my hand a light squeeze and says a few consoling words.

When the phone finally rings, I snatch the receiver from the operator's hand. It's a call from Matt Keller.

'Hi Abbey. What's the weather like in Jamshedpur?' he asks.

It must be Wednesday today, I think, forcing myself to respond. 'The weather is great here, Matt. I hope everything is all right with you.'

'I just called your parents to find out where I could reach you. They told me you were going for an alumni meeting at MIJ. It took us a while to get the telephone number. Let me cut to the chase, Abbey. When we gave you the task of restructuring the workforce in the factory, we weren't sure about your ability to pull it off. You started off rather mechanically and faltered. The first few separations were a disaster. But we saw that you were trying to operate within the framework of your own values. You came back to us with a proposal that was fair to both, the workers and the officers. That's when we knew we had a winner in you. I loved the idea of the milk cooperative that you came up with. A great example of Corporate Social Responsibility, as they would say back home in the US of A. In recognition of your contribution to rebuilding a new future for Gronier, we would like to offer you a job again.'

I am silent for a moment, Then I ask, 'What will I have to do, Matt?'

'A helluva lot. The board has passed a resolution to take you on as a director on the board of Gronier. We figured, making you a director would be the easiest way to get the average age of the board down! So from the first of January, you will be one of our directors. Congratulations, Abbey. The media would have picked up the news by now. I thought you should hear it from me first. I hope you'll throw a grand party for everyone at MIJ. And Abbey, get back here soon, okay? You will need to go to New York to meet the team.'

I hang up the phone and sit down on the chair next to the operator. It's too much to take in at once. My first reaction is of relief that my parents are fine. I look at Cauvita, who is trying to read my mind. When I smile, she smiles too, with a slightly puzzled expression on her face.

The phone rings again. The operator speaks into the phone with his eyes on me. Then he puts the phone down and turns to me. 'The editor of *Business Times* is looking for you. They want to feature you on the front page tomorrow. They want to be the first to break the news of your becoming a director on the board of Gronier. They are sending a photographer right away.'

'Hey, congrats! You never told me that you were on the board of Gronier. Or were you saving the news for this evening?'

I can't decide whether to tell her the truth or play to the gallery and pretend I've known all along. Before I can say a word, the phone rings again. It is Ma.

'Chotka, I cannot imagine you as a director. I have to go to Calcutta and offer special prayers to Kaali Thakur,' says Ma.

Asmita grabs the phone from Ma and squeals, 'Bhai, how big is your cabin? Here, talk to Baba.'

Baba asks me if, as a director, I can be put behind bars if someone files a case against the company, but Ma takes the phone away from him.

Suddenly, I am eager to meet the batch of '84. The main attraction for the evening is an audio-visual presentation the current batch of students at MIJ have put together. Cauvita tells me that it's a series of photographs of people from our batch set to music. I don't want to miss that.

Cauvita and I walk towards the lawns of the Institute. Every few minutes I meet people who were, and continue to be, an integral part of MIJ. Daadu's Dhaba is doing brisk business. His son Niranjan has taken over from Daadu. Posters of Madonna and Rocky adorn the walls. Niranjan tells me that the menu offers more options than ever before. Niranjan's mother, whom every MIJ-ite referred to as Didima, is still the driving force behind the institution. She recognizes me and yells out to Daadu to come over. Then she brings me hot jalebis on a saucer. Niranjan follows with a cup of steaming hot, syrupy sweet chai. When I pull out my wallet to pay, Didima and Daadu are truly hurt. Daadu asks me for a cigarette. I wait for him to finish smoking. Then I press a five-hundred-rupee note into Niranjan's hand. He asks if I might have a job for his younger brother. Monoranjan, he adds with obvious pride, is now studying in Calcutta. I nod. Daadu asks Niranjan with mock seriousness if there are any dues outstanding from the days when I was a student. Didima chides him for being cruel. She enquires if I have any kids and then tells me that it's high time I had one. I nod again.

I walk towards the main building where the party is about to begin. Someone comes from behind and thumps me so hard on my back that for a second I cannot breathe. I turn around to see a short, stout man, glasses perched low on his nose, laughing at me. He is carrying two grocery bags full of vegetables.

'You have obviaaslee not raycognized me. Even though statisticalee speaking, the probabilitee of a student recognizing a prophessar...'

'Professor Tathagato Chattopadhyay! How are you, sir? You have grown a beard. Do you need help with those bags?' I offer to help.

'I have just heard the news. I am very proud that there is at least one director of a company who understands

Quantitative Takeneeks! Hahaha! My wife steeel remembers how you came obhaar with that gaarl Keya to have ilish machher jhol. So, do you get time to see good films and read good books?'

I bypass all references to Keya and instead tell him how the death of Satyajit Ray is a void never to be filled. Professor Chatto leaves the scene a happy man and goes home after extracting a promise from me that I will visit him at home to see his latest series of paintings called 'Naked Tribal Women'.

Cauvita is a mute spectator to this display of bonhomie. It will probably take her more than a few minutes to recover from the shock of knowing that Chatto paints women in the raw.

She looks at me and says, 'Professor Chattopadhyay told me that you were one of the toppers of your batch.'

'He is probably confusing me with someone else – possibly Sethu, who topped our class. I barely scraped through.'

Cauvita puts her hand lightly on my elbow and says, 'You are kind of cool. I would love to chat with you some more, maybe after the party – if you are not too sleepy.' There is promise in the invitation.

'I would absolutely love to spend more time with you. Let me meet you after dinner,' I promise her. And I mean it.

I can hear familiar voices. Manjushri Gaekwad alias Mona Darling is standing under a tree near the Academic Block. She is dressed in a silk saree and sports a huge red bindi. Except for the few extra pounds that she has put on, Mona looks much the same. It's good to be back among friends. Mona was never a great friend of mine when I was at MIJ. Yet I feel a certain kinship with her that is difficult to explain. I had heard that she quit her job with one of the biggest foreign banks to start a school for the hearing impaired and has started a trust to support the education of slum children in Bombay. She is talking to Alpana alias Alps of the 'twin peaks' fame.

'Hi Mona Darling! Hi Alps! When did you guys get here?'

'Hi Abbey! Oh my God, you haven't changed. Have you been dyeing your hair?' squeals Manjushri.

'There's no hair left to dye. Hey Alps, I never thought you would end up making movies. That's so cool,' I say.

'That's the only way I could be the first in our batch to become a director! So I beat you to it, Abbey. Congrats on your appointment. Everyone's talking about it. By the way, Rusty and Funny have already started drinking. And did you know that Arunesh has quit his job to start his own rock band? That is so cool, to do something beyond the boring corporate sector. He has come with Piyu Walia, the playback singer. They have set up a stage in the Central Lawn and have a major concert planned for us.'

We walk towards the lawn where Arunesh and Piyu Walia are doing a sound check on the equipment. Rusty is dressed in a pair of jeans and a black shirt that is his trademark outfit. He is smoking a pipe, just the way he used to – only this one actually contains tobacco. I give him a bear hug.

'Rusty, you fucking stingy bastard. You never sent me an air ticket to visit you in Dubai. Hey, I never knew you drank alcohol.' I point to the glass of Scotch in Rusty's hand.

'I still don't. At every party I pick up a glass of booze and then discreetly pour it out when the guests have left. People don't understand why someone would choose to be a teetotaller. So it's easier to just blend in. Pappu was looking for you, by the way. I only hope that bugger has not gone to the room to sleep. He'll miss the party. Let me ask one of the students to go look for him.' Rusty stops to light his pipe. 'There is a surprise for you this evening,' he says.

I notice that he is smoking a brand of pipe tobacco called Three Nuns. I want to ask him what the surprise is, but someone taps me on the shoulder and distracts me. It's Funny alias Phanibhushan Grover.

'Bhayncho, where the fuck were you? I have been saving some Scotch for you – I am in charge of the bar this evening. Do you want to drink that or will you stick to OM2?' Funny loves playing the host.

'Where is Hairy?' I ask Funny.

'Hairy is now bhayncho Doctor Harpal Singh. He is teaching math in Colorado or some such place. That fucker got 1.38 in Chatto's class. The world is toh bhayncho crazy. Have you seen Gopher? He is giving career advice to the chicks of MIJ. What is worse, they are taking him bhayncho seriously.'

I wave to Arunesh, who's on the stage. He waves back.

'A big welcome to the batch of 1984 from MIJ – the batch that runs corporate India and now makes the best films, thanks to Alps, and also provides the masses with spiritual guidance, thanks to our very own Vishy... Come on everyone, let's hear some enthusiastic shouting! And now let's hear all those songs that we used to listen to when we were on campus. Shall we? Tonight I present live in MIJ, the one and only Piyu Walia.' Arunesh speaks like a seasoned rocker.

Piyu moves into a dance that's pure erotica. The audience screams and whistles. Pappu, meanwhile, has come up and is standing next to me looking mildly apologetic for being late. I punch his beer belly and tell him that it's okay. He smiles sheepishly.

There is serious drinking to be done. Gur and Neetika have joined us, as has Sethu. Gopher is dancing in the middle of the lawn, trying to attract attention. Joy and Fundu are having a conversation in the corner. Nanny is pregnant and cannot join us, says Pappu.

We are all drinking like it's going out of fashion. Daadu's Dhaba is doing brisk business and Didima is watching from the sidelines. They have made pakoras and noodles as part of a special menu. They wave at me. I go up to say hello and chat with them for a few minutes before coming back for another swig of booze.

A car pulls up at the gate. There is a murmur among the crowd and everyone turns to look at me. I am caught unawares. I wonder what I have done to deserve the attention. A familiar voice is the answer.

'Hi, everyone. Sorry I am late. The flight from New York was awful. The stopover at London took an extra two hours. Honestly, flying to India is such a pain. Hi Abbey! How are you, darling?' says Ayesha as she blows a kiss at me and comes over to give me a big hug.

She is wearing a designer gown like the ones you see in film magazines, with half of her back and seven-eighth of her breasts on display. So this is the surprise that Rusty referred to. I give her a lukewarm hug.

She mutters in my ears as she smiles for the world, 'Please don't make an ass of yourself, Abbey. Please at least pretend to be happy to see your wife. We are on stage. Congrats, darling, on your appointment as a director on the board. So do you drive a Mercedes now, or whatever is the equivalent available in India?'

I keep my arm around her and whisper back, 'I had no idea that you are MY wife. That was a just a role you played for a short while. You are Kevin's mistress.'

'You have a mistress too, Abbey. I believe Keya has conveniently stepped in to fulfill your needs,' Ayesha whispers before letting me go.

She looks into my eyes lovingly and slips an arm through mine. After a while the whispers die down and people concentrate on the music in general and Piyu in particular. I don't feel any anger towards Ayesha. I just that I don't wish to pretend any more.

'I've come to give you some good news. I've decided to go ahead with our divorce. So you are free to screw Keya without any feelings of guilt.' She says this without a trace of emotion crossing her face. Anyone would think she was commenting on the song that has just ended.

I empty my full glass in one shot, the way we used to in the WC-DMR contests. Then I give Ayesha a heartfelt hug. From the corner of my eye I notice Alps giving us the thumbs-up sign and a wink to say that she is happy to see us getting back together.

The best part about the reunion is that alcohol is abundant. We are all piss drunk and trying to dance to the old songs that Arunesh plays for us. He plays Dylan and Deep Purple's greatest hits. Finally someone shouts out a request for 'Diana's Song'. We all want to dance to that. I put my glass down and seize the arm of the first girl who comes my way. She is a student from the current batch at MIJ. We join the other drunk MIJ-ites on the dance floor. Arunesh clears his throat and launches into the much awaited song:

Diana, Diana show me your legs
Diana, Diana show me your legs
Diana, Diana show me your legs
A foot above your knee
Rich girl rides a limousine
Poor girl rides a truck

The only ride that Diana gets
Is when she is having a F...
Rich girl wears a ring of gold
Poor girl wears of brass
The only ring that Diana's got
Is the one around her...

Suddenly, Cauvita gets up on the stage and whispers in Arunesh's ear. He stops mid-song and there is a moment of confused silence before she takes the mike from him and announces in a voice choked with emotion that Father Hathaway has died in his sleep.

We all stand there stupefied, unable to absorb the news. Haathi is no more. It seems unreal. No one can imagine MIJ without Haathi. Gradually, in clusters of three and four, we make our way towards his room. There is a growing crowd of people waiting outside, where Haathi's body has been placed. One of the other priests, Father Malcolm, is keeping the crowd away. No one is crying. I don't think anyone can believe that Haathi is no more.

Father Malcolm addresses the crowd. 'May I request you to step aside and make way for the alumni from the batch of '84? Father Hathaway was writing individual notes for each one of them when he... gave up. I would like to hand the notes over as his last gift. The first envelope is marked for Mr Rustom Topiwalla.'

Rusty steps up, takes the envelope and breaks down. The dam has burst open.

One by one all the envelopes are distributed. I move away from the crowd and walk towards the auditorium as if in a daze. I sit on the steps and take out the letter addressed to me. It looks unfinished. It was clearly the last note that he wrote. Many years ago, when we completed our time at MIJ, he had written just such a note for each one of us. I still have mine tucked away among my most precious possessions. A letter I had read so often that the words were written into my memory, but it always reassured me to see them in Haathi's neat handwriting. As though he was talking to me in person.

I feel someone's hand on my shoulder. It is Cauvita. She is sobbing. I let my eyes follow the words in the letter in my hand:

Dear Abbey,

Today is the day to turn the clock back and think before you get washed away in the celebrations that happen when friends meet. There is much to catch up on and so much to share. So many bittersweet memories of the times spent together.

The first ten years at work are always eventful – personally and professionally. Whether it is success or failure, remember that 'this too shall pass'. The corporate world is full of illusions. Like all illusions, they are ephemeral. Power, money and in some cases even your relationships are not real. You are only as powerful as your last business card. Don't ever take the business card so seriously that it defines your entire identity and you feel helpless without it. Your career, like everyone else's, will have its share of disappointments. Those are the moments when you should ask yourself what you are disappointed about. Are you disappointed with yourself and your abilities, or with others? If it is the latter, maybe you are taking the business card too seriously. If you want success, think of yourself. If you want happiness, think of others.

Viktor Frankl used to say, 'What matters is not what you expected from life, but what life expected from you.' Stop asking about the meaning of life and instead, think of yourself as the one being questioned by life. Your answer must consist, not in talk and meditation, but in right action and in right conduct. Ultimately, you have to take responsibility for finding the right answers to life's problems.

As I read the last line, I know that life will never be the same again. I sit for a moment, rereading and absorbing the words. Then I turn and take Cauvita's hand in mine.

'Let's go find the others,' I say. 'The last thing Father would have wanted is to break up the reunion.'

Cauvita looks at me first in disbelief, then in recognition of my need to do something, to get out of the moment.

'Yes, let's go,' she says gently. It's time to toast the batch of '84 and the grand old man of MIJ.'

We link arms and step out into the night.